"You need to get yourself on the *____* ight out of here...."

Elisa had known *____* ____ *____* re it happened, and *____* ____ *____* d possessiveness *____* ____ *____* nds reached for him a*____* ____ *____* gment.

His mouth was so soft, so demanding, so giving. It made her cells sing with pleasure.

She was aware of her body, like a chant. Want. More.

His tongue urged her lips to open, and she let him in. The stroke of his tongue against all the tender bits of her mouth made her sigh. He groaned in response. That sound undid all her resistance, and she pulled his head down to get more of him. He tasted so good, of whiskey and wine and Brett. She knew this kiss, knew it inside and out, knew that he was going to bite her lower lip before he did, knew that he wanted her to meet his thrusts and that when she did she'd feel it down to her toes, that slide and urgency.

Want. More.

She did. She wanted him to pick her up and carry her into the room where—

Reason rushed in like an unwanted rainstorm. This could not happen.

She let go of his head and gently shoved his shoulder.

He looked back at her with lust-glazed eyes.

"Are you crazy?" she demanded.

Of course what she meant was, *Am I crazy?* Which clearly she was....

Dear Reader,

I've lived on both sides of the country, but have never managed to find a home someplace the sun shines in January. If you're suffering through gray, snow or cold, this is the perfect time to take a trip to the Caribbean for a dating boot camp with *Still So Hot!* heroine Elisa Henderson!

Elisa Henderson is a dating coach, and she's pretty sure she has the best job in the world. She gets to spend time with cool women, boost their self-confidence and teach them how to meet and keep the right man. I've written about people with all kinds of careers, but it's possible Elisa's is the most fun.

This weekend, Elisa gets to do her job on the beaches and in the bars of St. Barts. She has three days and three nights to teach TV celebrity Celine Carr how to find a healthier dating style.

If only it were that simple! En route to the airport, Celine Carr picks up a man—troublemaking, woman-collecting, soon-to-be-TV's-newest-news-anchor Brett Jordan, aka the man who broke Elisa's heart. Brett is one of my favorite heroes because he's a deep-down good guy who's spent so much time being bad he's lost track of his true self. I hope you'll have as much fun watching the sparks fly between him and Elisa as I had writing about them.

Happy reading!

Serena Bell

Still So Hot!

—

Serena Bell

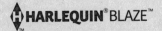

Recycling programs
for this product may
not exist in your area.

ISBN-13: 978-0-373-79785-1

STILL SO HOT!

Copyright © 2014 by Serena Bell

This is a work of fiction. Names, characters, places and incidents are either the product of the author's imagination or are used fictitiously, and any resemblance to actual persons, living or dead, business establishments, events or locales is entirely coincidental.

This edition published by arrangement with Harlequin Books S.A.

For questions and comments about the quality of this book, please contact us at CustomerService@Harlequin.com.

® and TM are trademarks of Harlequin Enterprises Limited or its corporate affiliates. Trademarks indicated with ® are registered in the United States Patent and Trademark Office, the Canadian Trade Marks Office and in other countries.

Printed in U.S.A.

www.Harlequin.com

ABOUT THE AUTHOR

Serena Bell writes stories about how sex messes with your head, why smart people do stupid things sometimes and how love can make it all better. She wrote her first steamy romance before she was old enough to understand what all the words meant and has been perfecting the art of hiding pages and screens from curious eyes ever since—a skill that's particularly useful now that she's a mother of two avid readers. When she's not scribbling stories or getting her butt kicked at Scrabble by her kids, she's practicing modern dance improv in the kitchen, swimming laps, needlepointing, hiking or reading on one of her large collection of electronic devices. Serena blogs regularly about writing and reading romance at www.serenabell.com and www.wonkomance.com. She also tweets like a madwoman as @serenabellbooks. You can reach her at serena@serenabell.com.

I'm thrilled to be working with awesome
Agent Emily, aka Emily Sylvan Kim of Prospect Agent,
and excellent Editor Dana, aka Harlequin's
Dana Hopkins, along with Copyeditor Ingrid Dolan
and Cover Designer Tony Horvath.

And none of this would be possible without the
unending support and love of Mr. Bell
and the two little Bells. *Hugs.*

1

ELISA HENDERSON HAD imagined worst-case-scenario headlines even before her plane took off.

Dating Coach Misplaces Client.

Client Goes AWOL from Dating Boot Camp in Caribbean.

God, this was *not* comforting. She needed to get up. She needed to move. Most of all, she needed to find out whether Celine Carr had made the flight. But she couldn't do that until the Fasten Seat Belt sign blinked off.

She'd gotten Celine's text just as Elisa had arrived at the gate. Thru security. Gotta pee. Board without me. She'd taken her seat in coach—alone, since Celine had claimed the last available in first class. Elisa tried to catch a glimpse of Celine, but the aisles were filled with other passengers. By the time Elisa had realized they were about to take off, she still didn't know if Celine was on the plane, and the flight attendants wouldn't let Elisa up. She'd tried to call and text Celine a million times, until a redheaded flight attendant pleaded with Elisa to put the cell phone away before she got them both in trouble.

Now all she could do was cross her fingers and try not to fidget.

Think positive. She's on the plane. She's raring to go.

This is the weekend you teach her that she calls the shots. That she controls her dating destiny.

This is the weekend you make hiring a dating coach the new black.

She took a few deep breaths and focused on positive visualization, which always helped her beat stress: Celine, sitting in first class, smiling and signing autographs, ready to make the best promo video ever. Celine, strolling the white-sand beach at the edge of the aquamarine Caribbean, hair blowing in the breeze, beside a handsome, attentive man. Celine, confident and competent, beaming her appreciation as she said to Elisa, *Thank you. You helped me see that I didn't have to keep making the same dating mistakes. The right man was out there.* Imaginary Celine tossed her hair, gave her guy a sidelong glance and linked her fingers through his. *Thank you for this wonderful man.*

Elisa loved the thrill of the match, the *click* of satisfaction she felt when she fit two people together like puzzle pieces. Plus, she *loved* running boot camps, intensive one-on-one weekends where she observed her clients in real-world dating situations and taught them new strategies. These weekends were a great chance to get to know a client well, learn her quirks and boost her self-esteem. And who could argue with a weekend in the Caribbean? Elisa was lucky that her sister's friend knew Celine's publicist, Haven, and had been willing to put them in touch. And maybe a little bit lucky, too, that Celine was already undergoing a major image revamp as Haven tried to halt her slide toward celebrity train wreck. It hadn't been *too* hard to convince Haven that a high-profile boot camp could turn Celine into a dating role model instead of someone whose antics reporters mocked. And if Elisa could make that happen for a rising star like Celine Carr, she'd have the added bonus of building her business's brand in a big way.

On the other hand, if Celine had missed the flight, Elisa would step off this plane into a barrage of firing flashbulbs and mocking voices calling out, "Where is she?"

Rendezvous Dating? Isn't that the business run by Elisa Henderson? The one who lost Celine Carr on the way to St. Barts?

She knocked her head against the back of the seat and closed her eyes.

The seat belt chime sounded. She unbuckled herself and hurried down the aisle.

"Whoa," said a deep voice, very close. She drew up abruptly to avoid a collision, and, for a moment, her mind was overwhelmed by a confusion of hands steadying her, a broad chest blocking her view and the smell of soap.

Then the voice said, "Lise?"

No. No. It wasn't possible. She knew that voice. Way too well. That voice represented a years-old friendship and B-grade movies and Chinese takeout and Scrabble games and that bar they'd gone to so often, the Aquarium…

The eerie light of that bar, a blue-tinged drunken haze, the stumbling walk home, her couch, his fingers in her hair, the taste of a mouth she'd longed for so badly she hadn't admitted it to herself, his tongue stroking hers, waking up every nerve ending in her entire body…

What the hell was *Brett Jordan* doing on her flight to the Caribbean?

She lifted her gaze and, unwillingly, took him in.

Dark hair, just long enough to be tousled. Harder-edged and squarer-jawed than he'd been at twenty-five. But cute, too—a vague upturn at the end of his nose, a slight cleft in his chin and the suggestion of dimples. He was the very definition of masculinity—and he wasn't much farther from her face than he'd been that night when he'd finally, finally lowered his lips to hers.

Two years hadn't quenched one ounce of the thirst. She could feel it, a sharp *want* that lit up all the tender parts of her mouth. She could feel it in her teeth, too. She'd nipped his lower lip that night, and he'd made a sound that didn't have a name.

She wanted to close her eyes and shut him out—and she wanted him to pick up where he'd left off.

Oh, of all the cosmic slaps across the face. No. Please no. Not him. Not now.

"Hi, Brett." Her voice sounded tight and unfriendly, even to her. Damn it. She'd been shooting for nonchalant, but she'd never been able to keep any part of herself in line when it came to him.

"This is wild!" he said. "What are the chances?"

Way too high, apparently.

"Well, you know," she said, with a shrug. *There. That'll show him.* He was the one who'd put the brakes on before anyone lost their pants, then *messed around with her sister less than two weeks later.* She'd never wanted to see him again, especially not on an airplane with no escape route and passengers peering up at them curiously. All this while the fate of her universe hung in the balance.

His grin was casual and disturbingly cute. "Are you going to St. Maarten? Or St. Barts?"

"St. Barts." She stepped to the side, nearly elbowing a seated passenger in the head. That was his cue to step to the other side, and they'd continue on their separate ways. He'd be grateful. No muss, no fuss, just the way he liked it.

But he didn't move from the middle of the aisle. His shoulders filled the gap between the seats so there was nothing for her to look at but the broad expanse of his chest. "Me, too. Catch me up, hot stuff. What's going on with you?"

He was talking to her as if it had been a few weeks since they'd seen one another, not two years. They hadn't just waved goodbye at their last visit and promised to get together soon. Their friendship had actually ended. It was as if he'd never kissed her, as if he'd never gone out with her sister. God, it galled her that he could pretend nothing had happened.

No, what really galled her was that, for him, nothing *had* happened. She'd been nothing more to him than a best buddy and an error in judgment.

The passengers around them had gone from curious to irritated, shifting in their seats and occasionally glaring.

"Another time, maybe." *Like never?* "I have to go talk to my client." And once again she feinted to the side, a more aggressive lunge. He'd have to get out of her way.

Instead, he stopped her with a hard hand on her arm. "You can't slip away *that* easy. What if you go into hiding for another two years? Are you still in New York? I am."

The presence of more than eight million people in the city of New York, where they'd both moved after college, made avoiding just one person easy. But hop a flight to a Caribbean island and blammo! There he was. Now that they'd run into each other once, she bet the island of Manhattan wouldn't be big enough to contain the two of them in isolation. She'd run into him in the grocery store every week now. That was how these things worked.

She was close, too close to him. She could smell him, old familiar scents that brought back half-forgotten longings. How could eau de Pert Plus shampoo and Old Spice cologne have such a profound effect on anyone? And that hand on her arm was like iron, a display of male strength on a scale she hadn't experienced in way too long. He was near enough that she could feel his heat, and longing slipped through her defenses and washed over her in a rush of sensation. She only prayed he couldn't see it on her face.

This was an act, she reminded herself—those pale green eyes so intent on her, the inviting grin, the banter—it was just habit, the way he was with women.

"There are no guarantees in life," she said. Miraculously her words came out cool and light.

He grinned at her. "See, I always liked that stuff you used to say. 'He who laughs last, thinks slowest.' And 'Where there's a will, I want to be in it.'"

He'd had that one crooked tooth on the bottom straightened since she'd seen him last. She missed the quirk of it. No, she didn't. She didn't miss a thing about him or their friendship.

The plane lurched slightly, and she grabbed on to a headrest. She was rewarded with raised eyebrows and a glare from the seat's occupant.

She tried to broadcast an apology, but the aggrieved passenger just turned away.

"We should get out of the aisle," she said. "I have to get to first class."

"You said your client's up there. What kind of client? Are you still working for that matchmaking company?"

"I have my own business now. I'm a dating coach. This is a one-on-one weekend dating boot camp. I watch her in action, give advice and basically play wingman—wingwoman—to her."

"So you're still doing it, huh? Making a career out of teaching women not to date me."

That ego! Unreal. Sure she'd harassed him about his wham-bam-thank-you-ma'am version of romance, threatening to tell the women of Carville College, and later the island of Manhattan, that Brett Jordan was not in their best interest. But that didn't mean he'd influenced her job choices

"I'm making a career out of teaching women not to date jerks," she corrected.

"Did you just call me a jerk?" He grinned.

Despite herself, she had to hide a smile. "You hear what you need to hear."

There was a brutal edge to the banter, and yet it felt familiar, very close to the old flirtation. She could miss that, too, if she weren't careful. This was exactly why she'd avoided all contact with him.

She shook her head. "Let's not do this."

"Do what?"

"Small talk, catch up—the whole *friends* thing. It's not a good idea."

The last trace of smile vanished. "I don't understand."

"I know you don't."

Behind Brett, the curtain veiling first class shifted and a vision of adorableness stepped around it, with shiny blond hair, big blue eyes, dimpled cheeks and a clingy purple dress totally unsuitable for plane travel. Celine.

Instantly Elisa felt better. Screw Brett Jordan and his burning gaze. That was then. Celine and Rendezvous Dating were now. "There she is." She made her voice light. "Hallelujah."

He didn't turn to look behind him. He kept his attention fixed on her. "The Facebook site. We'll catch up online. I'll friend you."

She needed to end this conversation now. And she needed to avoid him for the rest of their overlapping time on St. Barts. She prayed he wasn't also on his way to the island's singles resort where she and Celine were headed. Wouldn't *that* be the cruelest joke. She wanted him far away from her boot camp weekend. Far, far away.

Her heart pounded. It was not in her nature to be cruel, but this was self-preservation, pure and simple. She needed him gone, immediately. "No. No Facebook. No Twitter. No email. No nothing. I'm not interested in being your friend, virtual or otherwise."

An unexpected expression crossed Celine's face, where she stood behind Brett. Confusion. Concern. Celine touched Brett's arm, and he turned toward her, a smile on his face.

Elisa's internal warning system shifted into overdrive.

That wasn't just any smile. That was Brett's patented twenty-four-hour smile.

"Hey," said Brett to Celine. Affectionately.

Oh, shit.

Celine's face was tipped up toward Brett like a flower receiving the sun. "Wait a sec. You know Elisa?"

Elisa could only watch this terrible slowly unfurling

mess. With an audience. People had stopped trying to pretend they weren't listening. Elisa could see naked curiosity on a few faces.

Brett frowned. "How do *you* know Elisa?"

No one spoke for a moment, and Brett's eyes moved from Elisa to Celine and back again.

And then he got it.

"Oh, sweetheart," he said to Celine. "If you were trying to date a guy who isn't a jerk, you missed the mark by a mile."

2

CELINE LOOKED LIKE she'd been punched. She had a sweet heart-shaped face that made her appear younger than her twenty-two years, and her bottom lip trembled. Elisa turned on Brett, years of self-righteous anger reasserting themselves. "Do you have to *act* like such a jerk?"

In the seat behind Brett an older woman hid a smile, but Elisa felt no sense of triumph.

"Apparently," he said easily. He leaned back against the nearest seat, clearly enjoying himself. "I always was good at it." The occupant of the seat gave Brett a dirty look, but Brett couldn't have seemed more relaxed if he'd put both hands behind his head and kicked off his shoes. It pissed her off, not only because she was sweaty and stressed out, and he was the coolest customer on earth, but also because he looked so freaking good. Why were cocky asshole men so hot? It was just. Not. Fair.

She had to rein it in. Her attraction, her irritation, her temper. This was a disaster on so many levels, she didn't know where to start figuring it out. And their audience was turning against them, passengers starting to gripe audibly to each other. Drama was one thing, open conflict another.

She'd wanted attention. That was the whole point of this outing. But now things were totally out of her control. There was this—this *swerve*. She didn't want eyes on her as she untangled these knots. "We'll talk about this after the flight lands," she said, with as much authority as she could summon.

Brett shrugged. "There's nothing to talk about."

Celine watched them, her gaze moving from one to the other, as if the volley of words was visible.

"I'd like to know what's going on." Elisa crossed her arms.

Brett raised his eyebrows. "Ask your *client*."

"I thought there might be two sides to the story."

"There's no story." His expression dared her to push him. "Tell you what. I just got up to stretch my legs, but I'm perfectly happy to hang out here in coach. I'll take your seat, Elisa."

Celine opened her mouth once, closed it again, then managed to speak one word. "Brett?" She looked up at him, borderline pleading. Even through the haze of her own anxiety, Elisa's dating coach radar shot to high alert. *Desperate! Take it down a notch!* She tried to broadcast this with her gaze, but Celine wasn't looking at her. "I'm sorry," Celine whispered to Brett. Actually it was closer to a whimper. "I was *going* to tell you."

Brett shrugged. "Okay. That's great. I appreciate that. But you'll pardon me if this is just a little too effed up for me. I'm a tagalong on a dating boot camp weekend. What role did you have in mind for me?" He addressed the question to both women. "Fluffer?" He chuckled.

Elisa closed her eyes. It was either that or laugh hysterically.

"Br—"

The red-haired flight attendant stepped out of first class and glared at them. "You can't congregate here."

Elisa squeezed Celine's shoulder hard. "Hon, let's go sit, okay?"

The flight attendant's male counterpart—tall, dark and chiseled—appeared behind the redhead and put a hand on her arm. "Everything okay here?" he asked her.

He'd leaned close to ask it, closer than the situation required. *Alert! Chemistry!* Were the two flight attendants a couple? Or did he just wish they were?

"Please return to your seats."

The sharp command from the redhead snapped Elisa out of her romantic reverie. "We'll just—" Elisa began to say, tugging on Celine.

The passenger behind Elisa touched her sleeve. "Is that Celine Carr?"

"No."

"It is! It's Celine Carr. Guys, you were right!"

There was a flurry of activity as the passengers within earshot dug through their carry-ons, pulled out pens and notebooks, and shoved them toward Celine. Cell phones popped up above the seat tops and into the aisle, clicking with artificial shutter noises.

"Please," said the redhead. "I can't have you gathering in the front of the plane. You need to return to your seats."

The passenger who'd touched Elisa's arm turned to the flight attendant. "Can she sign autographs in the back?"

The female flight attendant cast an uncertain look at her colleague. He shrugged.

"It's Celine Carr! From *Broken*."

"What's that?"

"You don't watch *Broken?*" That was another passenger.

"Ohmigod, it's so good!"

Haven had warned Elisa that this would happen. Celine was a new star, not yet a household name, but she had a show that was rising in the ratings and people would recognize her, wherever she went. "As much of a pain as it is," Haven had said, "you have to let her do it. They're her fan base."

"If we stay out of the way?" Elisa asked the uniformed woman.

The flight attendant sighed. "Okay. Until we get the beverage service going, she can sign in the back. But make sure people can get to the restrooms."

A small shy smile had crept over Celine's face as she surveyed the outstretched hands clutching paper and notebooks and business cards.

"Give me a minute. We need to talk about this weekend," Elisa told Brett.

"I don't see what there is to talk about."

"You can't just—"

"Folks," the male flight attendant said in a stern voice.

"Come here a sec," Elisa said, starting toward the back of the plane. It wouldn't help her cause if she got them arrested for creating a disturbance on an airplane.

The fans followed, crowding into the back of the plane. Some startled bathroomgoers looked at them strangely, but others joined in, digging in pockets or squeezing through the throng to grab pens from their bags. Brett leaned against a galley wall, right behind Celine, frowning.

Still So Hot!

Elisa, heart still pounding, waited next to the red-haired flight attendant while Celine happily held court. Her loyal subjects produced napkins or their own arms for her to sign.

"Can you sign this for my daughter?"

"Can you write 'Love to Suze'?"

"Do you watch *Broken?*" the flight attendant asked Elisa.

Elisa nodded. "Do you?"

"I record it on TiVo." She was a pretty woman, with a smattering of freckles and a nice smile. "But we're never home, so we don't get to watch much TV."

We. "You and—?" Elisa gestured to the male flight attendant who was chatting jovially with a passenger just out of their earshot.

"What? No!" She laughed. "He's gay. 'We' is me and my roommate."

"He's not gay," said Elisa. "Trust me." Elisa pulled her business card from her pants pocket and handed it over. "It's my job to notice these things."

"Dating coach?"

"Yep. You want my suggestion?"

The flight attendant nodded, eyes eager.

God, Elisa loved her job. "Ask him if he wants to buy you a drink when you land. You'll see. He's not gay."

The redhead looked doubtful.

"My cell number is on the card. Text me and tell me what happens."

The flight attendant hesitated. "You sure?"

"Positive." Elisa would be willing to bet a thousand dollars they'd be lovers within a week. *If* the woman took her advice.

That was a big *if.* People were shockingly bad at doing what was best for them.

Like Celine, who had apparently acquired a traveling companion somewhere between yesterday afternoon—when Elisa had helped Celine pack her suitcase—and this morning when she'd boarded a plane for the boot camp weekend. *What had she been thinking?*

Papers and pens still shuffled across the galley, voices ringing out with questions for the actress.

"Is it true they're going to kill off Jonah?"

"Celine, will you have dinner with me?"

A voice rose from among the others. "Celine, who's the new guy? Hey, new guy—can you move in a little closer to Celine for me?"

All motion stopped, and there was an instant of total silence. Everyone turned to look at the person who'd asked that, a man whose face was mostly veiled by a black hoodie. And then they turned to look at Brett, leaning against the wall behind Celine.

Elisa opened her mouth, but before she could say anything, Brett pushed off the wall, took a threatening step forward and said, "Put that thing away."

Hoodie guy's mouth slowly tipped up into a smile, and he raised his hand. He had something clutched there, and for a brief, heart-stopping second, Elisa actually thought it might be a gun. Then she saw what it was and wished she'd been right in the first place.

Camera. Big camera. Real camera.

Paparazzo.

His smile got bigger as he began shooting, the shutter whirring as it squeezed off shot after shot of Brett and Celine.

THE LOOK ON Elisa's face, pure panic, spurred Brett to action. He slid past her, jostling other passengers out of the way, and lunged at the photographer, yanking the camera out of the guy's hands.

"That's personal property!" The guy grabbed for it, but Brett turned his back and ran his hands over the camera's casing, probing for the slot where the memory card lived. He found its catch, withdrew the card, dropped it to the floor and ground it into the carpet. The cheap plastic splintered. He closed the slot and handed the camera back to the photographer.

"Here's your personal property."

"What's going on?"

It was the male flight attendant, followed by a well-built guy in a business suit. Sky marshal, Brett would wager. Most of the other passengers had dispersed at the sight of this new authority. The flight attendant glared at both Brett and the hooded paparazzo.

"Nothing's going on." Brett looked around at the remaining passengers, daring them to disagree.

No one spoke up. His good luck—paparazzi were so loathsome that fear of the crazy man in the aisle paled in comparison.

The guy in the hoodie hadn't spoken.

"I'm going to need all of you to return to your seats, please," the flight attendant said sternly.

Brett shot a glance Elisa's way as she edged back toward her seat. The panic was gone, but she wasn't making grateful Bambi eyes at him, either. She looked pissed. He guessed he shouldn't be surprised. She was probably as bewildered by his intrusion into her boot camp weekend as he was to find that his old friend was a third wheel on his Caribbean getaway.

"Hey." He touched her arm, trying to soften her. "I meant what I said. Why don't you and Celine take the two seats in first class? I'll take yours. I'm sure you guys have some talking to do."

"There weren't two in first class when I tried to book."

"Last-minute cancellation. Or Celine's persuasive power." He shrugged. "Take the seats, okay?"

Elisa gave a tight nod. Man, she was pretty. He'd forgotten. Or made himself forget. She had hair the exact color of gingerbread and hazel eyes and the smoothest skin, like a porcelain doll. He still remembered the feel of that skin pressed against his cheek, under his lips. He craved it, nights when he was tired and weak. That and the weight of her breast in his hand, her nipple hard against his fingertips, her needy noises tracing a straight line to his cock.

He was getting hard thinking about it, and that meant less blood to the brain, which couldn't be good in a screwed-up situation like this one. *Concentrate, man,* he commanded himself.

"Let me get my stuff," Elisa said. "Celine, you head up front. I'll be there in a minute."

Celine went obediently, and Elisa practically shoved the guy in the hoodie out of her way. She bent down to retrieve something from her seat. Yeah, that was a good view of her, too.

"What the hell, man?"

For the briefest of instants, he thought it was the voice inside his head chiding him for ogling her ass, but then he realized it was the paparazzo snarling at him. Brett shrugged. "I'm sure you've got extras."

"I'm trying to do my job! You might not like it, but it's what I do, and those were my photos you smashed."

Brett could see the guy was one heartbeat from planting a hand in the middle of Brett's chest and shoving.

Let him try. Brett had enough aimless anger at the moment to flatten him into next week.

"Gentlemen, I need you to return to your seats," repeated the male flight attendant. "Unless you need a personal escort?" He nodded toward the sky marshal.

The paparazzo harrumphed like an angsty teenager and slunk away. The flight attendant and sky marshal eased against the seats to let him pass.

Brett headed toward the back of the plane. He met Elisa in the aisle, where she'd just finished hoisting out her carry-on. The top few buttons of her ruffled white blouse were undone revealing the delicate thrust of her collarbone and, below that, the swell of her phenomenal breasts. A wicked taunt—the ones that got away. Over the past two years, he'd managed to mostly block the memories of kissing her and touching her. Mostly, that is, except in his dreams. He dreamed about Elisa confoundingly often—languid, dirty, wet dreams. But this was real, because she wasn't slowly peeling off her clothes and looking at him with heat in her eyes, and she wasn't taking slow steps toward him, which was what always happened in the dreams.

"Sit for a minute." Elisa's words penetrated through his fog. He was lucky she couldn't read minds.

Her seat and the one beside it were empty—the other occupant must have been in the restroom. She slid in, and he sat beside her, hyperaware of the thinness of her blouse. He could see the hint of her skin beneath the translucent fabric.

"So, what?" she demanded. "You picked her up somewhere? And—"

"The drugstore," he admitted, before he could stop himself.

"You picked her up at a *drugstore?*"

She said it like he was dirt. She'd always been like this, judgmental about his conquests.

"She had one of those red baskets, and it was full of sample bottles. I said, 'Going on a trip?' and she looked up at me, smiled and said, 'Yeah. Wanna come?'"

And all right, he'd panicked. He'd looked at her pretty round face and her soft blond hair and her big breasts and he'd thought, *In two weeks, it's all over for me. No more women, no more conquests.* He'd promised the network where he'd just been hired on to be a news anchor that he'd be squeaky clean. Network anchors didn't chase tail. He'd barely beaten out his competition for this job, and his new boss had informed him that the other guy's advantage had lain squarely in the fact that he was older, more distinguished and well established as a husband, father and grandfather. The kind of guy you wanted to believe when he told you the news.

Brett, on the other hand—

Well, Elisa's unspoken assessment of him had probably been accurate. Women were his drug of choice and his downfall.

The truth was, standing in the drugstore, contemplating the vaguely familiar goddess in front of him, he wasn't sure he could do it. He wasn't sure he could be Mr. Squeaky-Clean Guy. Mr. Face of the News. Mr. Trust Me.

Pretty boy. Big man. Handsome, groomed, in control. That was who he'd been among his brothers—Zach had been the smart one, Pete the athletic one, and Brett was the good-looking one. It was what he'd traded on, with women, in his work, his whole life. Now he was here, on the brink of the anchor job, and if he couldn't do it…

Where did that leave him? If he couldn't be "the face of NYCN News"…

Screw that. Failure wasn't an option. He'd been prepping for an opportunity like this one his whole life, and he wasn't going to let *anything* get in his way.

Standing there in the drugstore, he had told himself that he'd accept this one invitation. Have a last hurrah, a crazy weekend with this very willing blonde bombshell. Then, he knew—he *knew*—he could do what the network needed him to do. He'd be ready to take on the world.

Elisa hadn't expected to hear that Celine had been the pickup artist. She shook her head. "And you said yes?"

"I said, 'I know you, don't I?'"

"Smooth."

He couldn't tell if she was admiring or mocking, but good sense dictated the latter. "It wasn't a pickup line. I didn't *need* a pickup line. She'd already invited me to the Caribbean. Although I didn't know yet that it was the Caribbean."

"God!" she burst out. "You're—"

But whatever she'd been about to say about him, she stopped.

He swallowed the urge to defend himself. He owed her nothing. He'd accepted a pretty woman's invitation to fly on the spur of the moment to the Caribbean for a good time. It wasn't his fault that the woman had neglected to mention she was in the middle of a dating workshop.

He'd had it all backward in the drugstore, of course. The window for a last fling, for getting women out of his system, had long since passed. He was already in the hot seat, already under scrutiny. Celine hadn't been an opportunity; she'd been a test. He'd had the chance to start his new life as Mr. Trust Me, and he'd screwed it up.

But maybe it wasn't too late. He'd made a mistake, but he could still right the ship and chart a new course. "Look. I'm outta here. I'll take the next flight back."

Elisa scowled. "You can't do that."

God, she was as bossy as ever. "I sure can."

She glanced around, lowered her voice. "Who saw you together?"

"What?"

"Who saw you guys together? In the airport. I've had a videographer following her around, but were there also paparazzi there? Are there photos?"

He shrugged. "Yeah."

"So you know what that means, right? Every entertainment magazine and show in the city'll have a piece on Celine and her new man—"

He couldn't help himself. He winced.

"Yes, that's you." She quirked her fingertips into quotation marks. "Celine Carr's 'New Man.' That's what you get for messing around with a celebrity. Finally found a woman you couldn't just slip into and out of unnoticed, huh?"

"Hey."

"Truth hurts?"

She was vicious. And he *liked* it. He liked her, eyes flashing, his old friend. He'd rather have her bitching at him than not talking to him any day. He'd *missed* her.

A thought came to him, unbidden. She'd be amazing in bed. The type who'd bite his shoulder and rake his back and yell when she came.

Not that it was an option. With that look on her face, it would be a cold day in hell before she'd have a civil conversation with him, let alone tangle with him in the naughty, uncensored way he envisioned.

And, really, could he blame her? He'd screwed things up royally back when he'd had his chance at her. He'd signed away his rights for all eternity.

Not to mention that, less than five minutes ago, he'd sworn off serial seduction. Hell, he'd sworn off women.

"If you leave now, they'll have a field day. They'll make mincemeat out of you, and Celine will come across as pathetic. You don't want that."

"So what's your point? I should stick around?"

"I'm saying that, if I were you, I wouldn't be in such a hurry to run off. There are more decorous ways to do it."

Decorous. Such an Elisa word.

"Let us get there, take some footage and photos of Celine doing her thing, make it clear that she's shopping around, not committed to you—then you split. Much less humiliating for both of you."

He could detect the hope and desperation behind her attempt at convincing him. She meant, *Much less humiliating for me.*

Her seatmate had returned from the bathroom and hovered expectantly over them. Time to go.

Well, okay, then. He could make this less humiliating for her. It would be a kind of penance, a chance to get back in her good graces. Not, he chastised his cock and all the other body parts clamoring for a piece of the situation, *those* good graces. But—

There was a chance, a small chance, he could make this better for her. Or at least *less worse.* And if he did, maybe they could be friends again. Because seeing her had reminded him of how much fun it had been to be friends with her in college and for the three years afterwards when they'd buddied around New York. How sometimes it had felt like the two of them against the world. Blowing off studying to eat pizza on the roof of the library, verbally dismembering their common enemies behind closed doors, stealing the Buddha statue from the religion department and installing it as guardian over the condom jar in the health center. She'd been funny, sharp, energetic, but kind, too, jollying him out of bad moods and dragging him on hikes in the New England mountains as an antidote to sophomore slumps and senior stress.

She was not the kind of friend who came along every day. There were eight million other people living in New York City, but no one played Scrabble with the focus or intensity that Elisa applied to the game. And of the other 7,999,999 New Yorkers, he had yet to find one who liked to deliberately pick bad DVDs and do her own *Mystery Science Theater 3000,* dissecting and mocking the films with glee. And no one had ever laughed at him with the utter abandon that Elisa had employed the day she'd taught him to Rollerblade, hoisting him up off the ground and then falling down beside him, breathless with hysteria.

You didn't get second chances too many times in life. "Okay," he said. "Fine. We'll do it your way."

3

ELISA COLLAPSED INTO the cushy first-class seat. "Okay. I think I talked Brett into not taking the next flight back."

There was silence from beside her, and she turned to discover that Celine was not awed and grateful, but confused. "He wanted to take the next flight back?"

Oh, man. She'd blown that. Why hadn't it occurred to her that Celine might still think a romance could develop between her and Brett? Brett always did manage to inspire unreasonable expectations in women. She of all people should know that. "He said the situation was too weird for him. You didn't mean to mislead him. It's just that he thought he was getting a special weekend with you."

"But you said now he's staying?" There was a sweet, hopeful note in Celine's voice. No wonder this woman got her heart publicly broken a minimum of five times a year. She had no hard-candy shell, only the melty center.

"Well, no—not staying. Just, I—" There was no diplomatic way to say this. "I thought it would be embarrassing for you if he left now, whereas if he stayed, we could make it look like you sent him away on your own terms. You guys can put on a nice show of having a destination date, and then you can decide you're not interested and move on. Everyone looks good."

Celine narrowed her eyes. "Everyone, meaning you?"

Elisa kept her irritation under tight wraps. "Everyone meaning everyone. Me, you, Brett. A more graceful exit for all of us."

"What if that's not what I want? A graceful exit?" Celine's voice rose.

"What *do* you want?"

"He said the situation was too weird, right? Because of the boot camp weekend?"

"Yeah."

"So let's do the boot camp weekend another time!" Celine was excited now. She pulled out her iPhone and tapped open her calendar. "I can't do the next three weekends, because I'm filming straight through, but I could do—no—I'm sure we could figure something out, though, right?"

"Hon—no. We've got a videographer here, I did a huge push in the media, and I can't get those people to take me seriously again if I bail now." The thought made her cringe. There were no do overs in PR. *No, for realz this time! Celine Carr's dating boot camp weekend!*

"Yeah. That would kinda suck. For *you*."

Ouch. Elisa didn't have to dig down far to read the subtext there. *But I'm paying you for this weekend, and you can sit down and shut up, if that's what I need you to do.* And Celine's unspoken chastisement was dead right. It wasn't Celine's job to win friends and followers for Rendezvous.

"You wouldn't have to go home. You could stick around and just be on vacation."

Elisa had to smile at Celine's stab at generosity. "Sure. I could."

"I'm just saying, Brett's only upset because you're still trying to match me up. He'd come around if you were out of the picture. And like I said, not totally out of the picture, just not so visible."

"If that's what you want," said Elisa, with effort. "We'll have to check in with Haven."

"Can we call her as soon as we land?"

"Yes."

Haven was supposed to be on this trip, too, but, at the last minute, her mother had been hospitalized with appendicitis. Haven had wanted to cancel the trip— "Keeping Celine Carr in line is a job for a paid PR professional"—but Elisa had promised that she could handle Celine. Elisa had assured Haven that she'd manage the media according to the publicist's directions, carefully watch out for Celine's well-being and call "the instant she sets a toenail out of line."

Haven was going to have rabbits when she heard that Celine had showed up for her flight with Brett in tow.

Elisa would worry about that later. She had bigger fish to fry right now, like making sure that her client didn't get her heart broken instead of having her self-confidence built up.

"Celine—" Oh, this was stupid and awkward. Whatever she said next would sound like sour grapes, but if she didn't say it, she'd be a really crappy dating coach. So, screw it, she'd rather be sour grapes than drop the ball. "I know you probably don't want to hear this right now, but Brett Jordan is—"

Well, who was or wasn't Brett, exactly? And what gave her the right to make that call? She'd had her own share of miscalculations about the kind of man he was. She was hardly an expert.

"What's the deal between you guys?" Celine's voice was sharp.

"There's no deal." She could see that Celine didn't believe her. Smart girl. "We were friends. There was a time, briefly, when I hoped—but there was never anything."

God, she was full of shit. *Never anything.* Nothing except kisses that had made her limp and golden and floaty, nothing except for his hands on her in a way that had made her willing to beg for more. And what exactly did she mean by telling Celine she'd been hopeful "briefly"? Briefly, if briefly meant all through college and for years after that. Even now she wasn't sure what she had wanted from him. Not anything he could give, that was for sure.

"So you were in love with him," Celine said.

"Not in love with him, no, I wouldn't— It was a long time ago. We were friends. He was—he dated a ton of women, just not me."

"But you're not objective."

The night Elisa had met Brett, he'd come wandering through the dorm looking for someone to play Scrabble with. She'd leaped at the opportunity. He was cute, with pale green eyes, an intense gaze and symmetrically hewn features, but she'd mostly been grateful to find someone who was as much of a word nerd as she was. He had known all the two-letter words in existence, had produced seven-letter words multiple times per game and had constantly manufactured crazy plays, laying one word alongside another to spawn five new words for thirtysomething points.

"I have an embarrassment of *O*s," he had said midway through that first night, turning his tile holder to face her. There they were, four *O*s in a row, lined up. "They're like four eyes, staring at me."

Back then, he had longish hair that fell over his face, and he shook it away periodically in a gesture that was too self-conscious for her taste but had made her palms a little sweaty anyway. "Only—they're *O*s, not eyes."

His own eyes had sparkled and a dimple had appeared in his cheek.

She'd started to laugh helplessly and he'd joined in. They'd stopped, gasping, and then started again until they rolled on the floor, and he'd said, "You're the best Scrabble partner I've found since I've been here. Will you play again? Will you play whenever I want?"

She'd shrugged, and because she had pride, she'd said, "When I feel like it," but in her heart, she'd known she'd always play with him.

That night she'd been pretty sure he felt about her the same way she felt about him. There were moments of prolonged eye contact and real flirtation, and when he had boxed up his game and gotten up to go, there was a long, awkward silence that afterward she thought of as a kiss that hadn't happened. Over the next few weeks, they had become friends, playing Scrabble almost every night, roller-skating, seeing movies, frequenting the same drunken parties, studying together. Nothing had happened between them, and soon she had begun to understand Brett's pattern. He liked to date beautiful women. Not cute or pretty or striking in an unusual way, but model-beautiful, the handful of women at their college who were truly glamorous. Or maybe "date" wasn't the right word. He had collected them. He had wooed them and had worn them on his arm briefly and let them pass out of his life again, as though they were bits of flotsam floating by on a river.

She had watched, and she had alternated between ferocious envy and gratitude that she wasn't the one being used and discarded.

From the first moment Brett Jordan had strolled down the dorm hallway with his Scrabble game in hand and poked his scruffy, beautiful head into her room, she hadn't been objective.

She wouldn't lie about that, not to herself and not to her client.

She looked up and saw with a jolt of relief that the flight attendant was headed toward them with a tray of champagne flutes. That would improve things. Not that they could really get much worse.

She collected two flutes from the tray and handed one to Celine. "No," Elisa finally answered.

And when Celine tilted her head quizzically, she shook her own and said, "You could safely say I'm not objective about Brett."

4

"CELINE! CELINE!" PAPARAZZI and reporters shouted.

Elisa was still reeling from the bumpy and terrifying descent onto the St. Barts's airstrip. It would be way too generous to call this an airport. Runway ten—the pilot had referred to it with affection, for reasons she couldn't fathom—ended in a shock of white beach and aquamarine water.

He'd warned them that the plane's safety system would protest the landing, but that didn't stop Elisa's heart from practically fleeing her chest when he dived over a hill and the warning system blared "Pull up!" She'd held her breath for the entire length of the runway while brakes squealed and flaps flapped, convinced that they'd miss the runway and land either on the highway or in the water. She'd been sure they'd have to climb out of the sea to start their trip.

"Celine!"

Elisa counted maybe ten yammering entertainment buzzards. Pretty good for a minor celebrity, and she felt a twinge of pride. They were here because of the buzz she'd made.

And then the pride deflated like a leaky balloon.

What a waste now, thanks to Brett.

They'd disembarked the plane into a brilliantly sunny, warm paradise, with white sailboats in the harbor, red-roofed houses dotting green hills and palm fronds waving in a light breeze. It had taken them just a few minutes to clear customs and collect their baggage, and now they stepped out of the protective atmosphere of the single-gate airport and into Celine's world. Media and clamor.

"Celine! Tell us why you're doing this! What's a weekend dating boot camp?"

No—Elisa wouldn't let her work be a waste. She would find a way to make the most of this moment. She'd come this far, and she was not going to back quietly away. Until the weekend was over, this was her show, her chance.

She and Brett and Celine pushed through the minimob. She kept a hand on Celine's back, moving her forward. Haven Hoyt had carefully coached Elisa on managing this moment.

"Don't stop walking or they'll pin you," Haven had said. "And for God's sake, smile. Every single second is a photo op, and the last thing you want is a photo of you with a grimace on your face plastered all over the internet."

They were almost to the cab, a soft-top Jeep Wrangler, a tough-looking jungle car in a sea of cutesy Smart cars. The cab would ferry them straight to the hotel, and then hotel security would take over the work of holding the media off Celine. Elisa's smile was starting to hurt, but she remembered Haven's words and kept it in place.

A microphone crowded her face. "Where'd they meet?" It was a blond woman Elisa vaguely recognized from the evening entertainment shows.

"On the town." Ooh, she was pleased with her answer. So much better than "in a drugstore."

"Were you with her?"

"She did it herself, using techniques I taught her. Teach a woman to fish…"

Laughter from the peanut gallery. That was good, right? Her smile was real now. Out of the corner of her eye she spotted her videographer, Morrow, hanging back from the pack, and he gave her a thumbs-up. She liked him a lot, and his previous clients, including some heavy hitters, had raved about his work.

The blond woman was a bulldog. "Is it serious?"

What had Haven said? *Every question is an opportunity.* "They've only known each other a few days. But who knows? If things go well, maybe she won't need me after this weekend."

More laughter. She looked over at Celine who was smiling brilliantly. Brett's expression didn't match. But he was a guy, so instead of looking grim, he looked serious and thoughtful. Authoritative.

That jaw. The fact that he hadn't shaved this morning made her want to test the texture of his stubble with her tongue.

Her smile had slipped slightly, and she tugged it back on.

"If she's only known him a few days, why'd she bring him to the Caribbean?"

Excellent question. I wish I knew. "Destination dates are becoming very popular. Rendezvous encourages its clients to pick exciting locations even for first dates. And of course Celine will meet many men and have a whole variety of dates this weekend."

She'd even gotten her business's name in without sounding like a total tool. They were at the Jeep, sliding across the backseat, Celine, then Brett, then Elisa, and the relief was as profound as if they'd entered a decontamination chamber. She slammed the door behind them, and the cab pulled away to a chorus of flashes.

"You were great!" Celine said.

"Very smooth." Brett's tone was so dry that once again she couldn't tell if he was mocking her.

She snuck a look at him. In the center seat, he'd leaned toward the windshield and was staring out at the green, brown and blue world. The road was narrow, and people kept squeezing past them in the opposite direction at ungodly speeds. She could blame the rapid trip of her pulse on that, not on the hard length of his thigh pressed against hers.

If he leaned back, his shoulder would trap hers against the backrest. When she'd ridden in cabs with him years ago in New York, the middle seat had kept a safe foot of distance between them.

She was breathless from triumph and hurrying across the tarmac, not to mention the scary driving. The amount of space Brett took up in the cab had nothing to do with it. Neither did the heat pouring off him or the scent of fresh male sweat and that still familiar Old Spice.

She certainly wasn't breathless from imagining what that hard thigh would feel like, eased between her s, or because she could remember the exact silken slip of his tongue against hers.

He's your client's date.

She inched toward the window until there was a narrow strip of space between their bodies. And began to work on slowing her breathing.

Her phone buzzed in her pocket. She pulled it out. The text was from an unknown number.

He said yes! (This is Sherry fr plane. Flight attndt.)

A big grin spread over Elisa's face.

Of course he did. Have fun!

Her phone buzzed right away.

THK U.

Keep me updated.

IOU

Give my card to a friend who lives in NYC.

Will do.

"You text fast," Brett observed.

Elisa laughed. "Sometimes people desperately need advice in the middle of their dates. I have, like, three seconds to tell them how to keep the date going or end it ASAP. Texting fast is a career skill."

"What kinds of things do they ask?"

I wore granny panties! What do I do if he wants to come in? "Oh, like, 'Should I let him pick up the check?'"

"And what do you say?"

Go to the restroom and take them off! "'There are no rules. Go with your gut.' Or 'If he offered, yes.'"

"Not, 'For God's sake, woman, don't do it! He's probably a jerk, and if you let him pay, he'll expect sex'?"

She glared at him and resumed paging through her texts. The next one was from Haven. How's it going?

Great so far. Didn't have to wait for cab. On way to hotel.

The phone vibrated in her hand. Glad to hear it.

Can I call you when I get to the resort? Slight complication. Pretty sure I've got it under control, just wanted a second opinion.

I'll be here.

The Jeep zoomed by a small cluster of shops on the right. She was surprised to find the island dustier and less jungle-verdant than she'd been expecting. Not Hawaii—spikier, more arid and windier—but beautiful nonetheless, even with vines and strange succulent plants that looked like they might eat people.

"So what's the plan, Queen of Hearts? How long do I stick around?"

"Elisa's going to take off. So you and I can hang out." Celine smiled her glossiest television smile.

She felt Brett's surprise. For a moment she let herself enjoy his discomfort. Served him right for picking up celebrities in drugstores and agreeing to fly to Caribbean islands with them. Served him right for—

She had to stop hating him. It was such an impediment to getting over him. She needed to feel nothing. Blank, neutral, maybe a mild irritation, like you'd feel at a housefly that had gotten into your kitchen.

"Celine said she'd like to postpone the boot camp weekend."

He frowned at Elisa, then turned his head to speak to Celine. "Look."

Oh, God, this was *exactly* what she'd been trying to prevent.

"Celine. You're a sweet girl. And this is an awkward situation."

He sounded so warm. So smooth. She'd never actually heard him dump a woman before, but it didn't surprise her that he was as skilled at it as he was at making conquests. Why not? He had abundant experience with both.

"If the circumstances were different, I'd love to get to know you better. Take our time. But this is just—" His gesture encompassed the three of them, the cab, the whole island. The paved road gave way to something bumpier, narrower and altogether less civilized. "This is bad juju. You're better off letting Elisa show you the ropes. There's a whole island waiting for you out there, and loads of men who are nicer than I am. Take my word for it."

Had every woman he'd slept with and dumped gotten this speech? Elisa should be thankful she'd been spared. Maybe walking away from their friendship had been the smartest move she could make. It certainly seemed like genius now.

Celine shifted uncomfortably. Elisa had never realized exactly how small a Jeep could feel. Though—as another car sped by and nearly took off the side of their vehicle—not small enough.

He hadn't left Celine any wiggle room. It was kind of brilliant, if you admired it coldly from the outside. What could Celine say, really?

Huh.

Then Elisa knew. Ha! Perfect answer. Not that she could convey it to Celine in the confines of the cab—no way to do *that* discreetly.

What Celine *should* say was *Actually? Nice isn't my thing.*

Of course, if she *did* say that—and in a tone of voice pitched somewhere between matter-of-fact and mildly suggestive—Elisa would have to throw herself out of the moving cab, because at that point she wouldn't be the ref in a boxing match, she'd be a dry log caught in the middle of a conflagration. Because that comeback would *definitely* catch Brett on fire. She couldn't have said how she knew it, but she *knew* dirty talk was one of his buttons.

Sometimes, during their friendship, she'd heard come-ons and rejoinders in her head—naughty, flirty words, a hard pressure behind her tongue. Sometimes she'd wished she were a little drunker so she could let them slip out and pretend they were a mistake. She'd wanted to watch the heat rise, see the flare of lust in his eyes. Then she could have let her gaze drop to measure how much her words had affected him.

But always the next morning she'd been glad she hadn't. And by evening she'd been gloriously thankful, as she watched him make yet another conquest, the starting gun for one more twenty-four-hour relationship.

For all those years, she'd been so careful, knowing that if she ever said the words that popped into her head, if she'd pushed the buttons, if she'd unleashed the heat she sensed in him, she'd only have become another twenty-four-hour girl.

And then that night, the night he'd kissed her, she'd let down her guard. She'd felt the precipice, and she'd hurled herself off it. And she'd gotten exactly what she'd known she would. He'd made her into yet another conquest. Only she hadn't even lasted twenty-four hours. More like twenty-four minutes, if that.

Beside her, Celine sighed. She lowered her head, stared out the window and said, "Yeah. Okay."

Elisa risked a glance at Brett. There was a small smile, something like triumph, on his face. And behind Elisa's tongue, desire that she bit back and swallowed.

5

BRETT SHADED HIS eyes with his hand. Nice scenery. Lush foliage and big tropical flowers and a horizon pool, built to look as if the water went straight on forever. The pool was the same blue as the cloudless sky.

The air was warm but not oppressively hot, and a light breeze blew now and again. He was glad there were some wispy clouds in the sky—otherwise, he wouldn't believe the scene was real. The resort was unbelievable—gorgeous rooms with white linens, flowers on the credenza and an orchid on the pillow. Thick plush towels in stacks in the bathroom and a white bathrobe behind the door. Flowers and palms and secluded little alcoves with marble benches. And an army of people employed to keep him happy. He'd just have to keep his mind off the tab and enjoy it as long as he could. Until Elisa ousted him from paradise.

Oh, yeah, and then there was the *other* scenery—a veritable army of bikini-clad women lying on chaises, sipping drinks, lounging on the steps in the shallow water. His mouth was dry, and he wasn't sure if it was the visuals or the fact that a G&T would be perfect right about now. All he'd have to do to get a drink was to flag down one of the many poolside waiters with trays on their hands and towels over their arms.

Because Elisa had said they should continue this half-assed charade, Celine had come down to the pool with him and was asleep face down on the chaise beside him, her cheek probably imprinted by now with the texture of the chair. He cast a wary glance in her direction. He'd promised to wake her if she slept too long so she could put on more sunscreen. "Celine."

She didn't move.

"Celine?"

He sighed. He didn't want to be responsible for burning America's newest sweetheart to a crisp. But he didn't want to wake a sleeping lionness, either. She'd been angry since his rejection in the cab.

Now she looked like a little kid, her mouth slightly open, her smooth, unlined face even more youthful in repose. She was definitely a wakeup call to him. Even though she was just five years younger than he and Elisa, she came across as far more naive.

He'd discovered there was a limit to how far even *he* would go, and picking up a twenty-two-year-old newbie TV star in a drugstore and following her to the Caribbean had showed him a set of lines he no longer wanted to cross. He'd had to ignore warning sirens in his brain to get himself here, and he wouldn't do that again. So the scenery might be lovely at this swimming pool, but until further notice, his policy was *look but don't touch*.

He was staring at one of the sunbathers when he discovered that she was Elisa. He hadn't done it with any kind of conscious thought; he'd just let his eyes drift until his attention had been snagged by a woman's golden limbs and reddish hair. It was always long legs and auburn hair that felled him. He would daydream, notice a woman and then realize he'd been half hoping it was Elisa. Only in this case it was, and instead of his heart sinking with disappointment, he felt a small hopeful glow in the center of his chest. She looked up just then, caught his eye and waved.

Damn it, he didn't like to be found staring. Men should avoid that at all costs. There was a fine art to scoping. You never let a woman see the top of your head or wonder where your eyes had been. A close outside observer might be able to read your mind, but the recipient of the gaze should never discover that it was directed at her unless you wanted her to. And he didn't want Elisa to know. Not by a long shot.

She'd gotten up from the lounger and was headed in his direction. Her long strides ate up the pebbled surface of the pool deck.

"Hey," she said.

She wore what should have probably been the dullest, drabbest bathing suit on earth. It was chocolate brown, with wide straps and a high heart-shaped neckline that curved over the tops of her breasts, and it was almost straight across the bottom, like high-cut shorts instead of a bathing suit triangle. But it wasn't drab on Elisa. The brown set off her eyes, and made the strands of red and gold in her hair stand out, and the cut of the suit—whatever the girly fashion name for it would be— reminded him of a '40s movie star and was somehow sexier for not trying to be flashy.

It looked like it would be a bitch to get her out of, but the finest pleasure, too. Like peeling fruit, exposing bare, round, luscious bits of her.

Now his mouth was *really* dry. "Hey."

She looked uncomfortable, her eyes not meeting his. "Is she—?"

"She's asleep."

Elisa knelt at the side of Celine's chaise, then nodded to confirm Brett's diagnosis. He made a superhuman effort not to stare at the neckline of Elisa's suit and the mouthwatering body it outlined. He tried to forget he knew the exact curve and weight of her, the way her lips parted when he touched her just right. *Those sounds she made.*

Instead he asked, "How long do we perpetuate this pretend romance?"

She stood up. "I just got off the phone with Celine's publicist. I needed another opinion."

"And did you get one?"

"She's good with the plan."

"Which is?"

"A couple of hours lounging at the pool together and a few drinks in the bar afterward. And then Celine moves on, and you're free to go." She surveyed the landscape of human flesh. "If you can drag yourself away." She chuckled.

He ignored that last line. "Will she cooperate?" He gestured at Celine. Awake, she'd been sullen and hostile, snapping at his attempts to make conversation and refusing his help to drag an empty chaise out of the shade.

"I'll tell her she has to. And Haven will tell her she has to. And it's just a few drinks. How much trouble can she cause?"

He shrugged. It made him uncomfortable to have Elisa towering over him, so he got to his feet. He'd forgotten how tall she was, only a couple of inches shorter than him. He liked tall women because he didn't have to stoop to kiss them.

He had to stop fantasizing about kissing her, about stripping her out of her clothes, about laying her on a chaise and sliding his body up the length of hers. He'd made the decision on the plane that, if he wanted to be her friend, he couldn't afford to remind her of what she hated about him. He couldn't be the man she'd built her whole career around outwitting. He'd shut that part of himself down.

Shut it down. Just like that.

Except he was still thinking about kissing Elisa. With a slight incline of his head, he could have those soft lips against his. And coax her tongue—

He knew exactly how it would feel against his. Like that night, when he'd wanted it to extinguish the craving, and instead it had fed the fire.

What was wrong with him, that he couldn't put sex out of his head for ten minutes?

She shifted from one foot to the other, hands on hips, which only made her waist look narrower. "So do you have a return flight?"

She'd lowered her voice, and, as if by agreement, they took a few steps away from where Celine lay.

"Haven't booked one yet. Have you tried to do anything online? Someone said it was insanely expensive to call out if you don't have an international plan, so I was trying to book through the website, but I couldn't get my laptop to connect to the hotel wireless—"

Elisa frowned and scraped a toe over the glossy surface of the pool deck. "You should get on that. I can do it on my phone if you can't get online."

"First you tell me I can't leave, and now you're trying to boot me off the island."

"I'm just—"

"You want me when you want me, and then you're done, and you kick me to the curb like I'm garbage—"

"I'm—" But then she got that he was messing with her and smiled. It made him miss the good old days with a vengeance. When they'd smiled at each other all the time, joked and laughed and flirted and—

For a long moment her eyes stayed on his face, as if she were thinking it, too, but just when he wasn't sure how much longer he could hold her gaze, it flickered to something behind him. He turned to look. All he saw was the spiky greenery at the side of the pool. Then his vision resolved a blur of floral color into a Hawaiian shirt on someone holding a long-lensed camera.

"Is that your guy?"

"No. Crap. It's the guy from the plane."

"Great. How long has he been standing there?"

"I don't know. He might have just showed up."

From where they were standing, they couldn't hear the whir of the digital shutter, but Brett knew he had to be shooting. It was too good an opportunity. The two of them, conspiring over the prone body of the sleeping TV star. "Do you think he heard any of our conversation?"

She eyed the distance between them and the burst of color in the foliage. "Probably not."

"So it's all visual. Stick out your hand. Like you're shaking mine. Look businesslike."

"Isn't it a little late for that?"

"Probably. But we can at least not give him any more raw material for scandal, right?"

She stuck her hand out, and he took it. Her hand was small, slim and surprisingly soft. She was angular and regal, but she still had that ultrafeminine, satiny feel to her skin. He wanted to rub his thumb over the back of her hand, over her wrist and up the inside of her arm. He wanted to see if the rest of her was as ridiculously soft and sweet. As her cheek. As her mouth.

Man, he was despicable. She was right about him. She'd always been right about him. And she'd been altogether right to get herself out of his life, because if she'd stuck around, he would have found a way to get in her pants. And there was no reason to think he'd have treated her any differently than the other women he'd discarded.

He'd proved it by running out on her that night and again two weeks later with her sister. God, he didn't like to think about that.

He was still holding her hand. She took it back and said, all business, "Good luck with drinks."

"Thanks."

"If you're lucky, you won't see me again, except maybe the back of my royal blue bathing cap as I do lengths of the pool." She waved, then turned.

"Okay."

But it wasn't okay. Not at all. She pivoted to walk away in earnest, and he checked out the bathing suit from the rear angle, that admirable contrast between the curve of her ass and the narrowest point of her waist, and hoped his bathing trunks weren't obviously broadcasting his admiration.

He hadn't actually *said* he'd leave after he ended his "relationship" with Celine. He hadn't looked up earlier flights home, and he didn't want to. It would be the gallant thing to do, of course. He should walk away and let Celine turn the weekend into a triumph. And it would be the prudent thing to do. The network was already going to be ticked at him for getting himself in the spotlight and not in a "family man" way.

But as he cursed that stupid, old-fashioned bathing suit, and its unexpected effect on his brain and cock, he knew one thing for sure. He wasn't ready to have Elisa Henderson walk away from him for good, and he sure as hell wasn't going to walk away from her.

6

SHE LAY ON the bed in her room. Decompressing. She had slipped into her nightgown to get out of her travel-worn clothing, and because the cool breeziness of the fabric felt good against her hot skin.

There was still a little light in the sky, and she could see the ocean through her open sliding glass doors. She'd consumed most of the room's gift basket, passion fruits and kiwis, in a frenzy of stress-eating that she'd had to follow up by drinking the orange juice from the minibar.

She'd tucked herself under the bed's lightweight white quilt and plumped herself up on a stack of feather pillows. So this was how the other half lived. She'd grown up in a small ranch house and shared a bedroom with her sister, their mother running her accounting business out of the other bedroom. Her mom had worn sweats 80 percent of the time, changing only when clients came to the house and did business at the kitchen table. Elisa had never learned to tell a salad fork from a shrimp fork, much less slept under Egyptian cotton sheets. She was hardly the poster child for someone who should be trafficking in image, celebrity or luxury.

But she kind of liked it—the horizon pool, the over-eager staff, the flowers and tropical fruit, and white-tiled hotel room floor. She could get used to this, provided Brett behaved and the rest of the weekend went as planned.

She used her smartphone to clean out her email in-box and listen to her voice mail. There was a message from one of her clients, a third-grade teacher. Elisa grinned as she heard Savannah's giddy voice. "Oh, my God, it was such a good date. I really, really like him, and he kissed me, and seriously you are my fairy god-mother. I can't wait to see you on Tuesday and tell you the whole story. I'm totally not telling it now, because I will clog up your voice mail, but we had such a good time and you were totally right. A jazz club was a way better choice than a movie. We could talk, and he kept leaning close to tell me funny things! Thank you, thank you! See you Tuesday!"

That was what she loved. The joy in Savannah's voice. The rib-crushing hug Savannah would undoubt-edly give her at her next appointment. The details Sa-vannah would dish over tea and shortbread cookies. And good first dates often led to good second dates and on down the line. Elisa couldn't start writing Savannah's wedding toast yet, but she'd been to nearly thirty cli-ent weddings now, and almost all of those couples had had great first dates. Elisa liked to save the voice mails to replay for her clients when they came in to display their engagement rings. She saved the message, then switched over to read an email that popped up.

It was another Facebook friend request from Brett. She'd refused at least five of his in the past two years. Each one had been an unpleasant tweaking reminder that he still existed. Somehow, despite her refusals, he remained stubbornly optimistic that she'd want to be "friends."

She deleted the request. She was softening toward him despite herself, and the last thing she needed was to see his face and his news every day.

She texted her sister, Julie. You won't believe this. Guess who Celine picked up en route and brought to the Caribbean?

george clooney?

Hint: The one topic we never discuss.

Long pause, then, brett???????????
Elisa's phone rang.

"How does that even happen?" Julie demanded. Her sister's voice, warm and familiar, was a welcome comfort. It was a miracle that what had happened with Brett and Julie had not poisoned the sisters' relationship. Elisa thanked God for it all the time. And she thanked God she'd told her sister, that night before Julie had gone out with Brett, "Whatever happens, I don't want to hear about it. Not a word." Because she knew there was no way in hell she could stand it. It was only the not-knowing that had made it possible for her and Julie to go on as if nothing had happened.

"I think I'm being punished," Elisa told Julie.

She explained the whole situation, from the long moments of worrying that Celine hadn't made the flight, to the drinks date going on in the resort bar at this very moment.

"Does he know how important this is to you?"

"I think so."

"Tell him if he screws this up for you *or* Celine, I will *kill* him."

Elisa loved her sister's ferocious protectiveness and wished for the ten-millionth time that Julie lived in New York with her and not on the other side of the country in Seattle. "I'm not worried. Brett's on board. He'll finish up with her, and then I'm going to take over, and we're going to have so much fun she's going to be too busy to get into trouble." She knew she sounded like she was trying to convince herself—she *was* trying to convince herself—but she had to stay positive.

"If anyone can do this, you can. I wish you'd been a dating coach when I was a teenager."

Julie had spent most of her high school years throwing herself recklessly into relationships with popular older boys and then weeping and sulking through dinner when, inevitably, things didn't work out for her. Elisa had rarely been able to use the home phone because Julie always tied it up crying to her friends. It was beyond Elisa how Julie could make the same mistake over and over again, but the pattern had continued to the present day.

It was possible, Elisa sometimes thought, that she'd become a dating coach partially to alleviate the frustration of watching helplessly as Julie flung herself against a brick wall, but of course she'd never told her sister.

"You just say the word, Jules. I'll drop everything and work with you."

"You've got bigger and better things going on." If there was any hint of sadness in her voice, it was overshadowed by her clear pride in Elisa's work. "Next week, your phone'll be ringing off the hook."

"Your mouth, God's ear." She was tempted to knock on wood.

Julie sighed. "I should let you go. You've got a long evening ahead of you, huh?"

"Yeah. Glad you called, Jules."

"Good to hear your voice, Lise."

"Love you."

"You, too."

She set the phone on the night table and collapsed back on her throne of pillows. For the first time today, she was alone and not desperately trying to fix this star-crossed weekend. The lack of imminent disaster felt glorious. Across the resort, Celine and Brett had met for their fake destination date, and that would close the door on all this silliness. Brett would fly home, and she and Celine would do their boot camp weekend, and maybe, just maybe, everything wouldn't fall apart. This could still become a victory for Rendezvous.

Her business was so new. She had a great start, but her ambitions were even grander. Eighteen months ago, things had been different. She'd been a cog in a wheel, a senior "relationship guru" at a matchmaking franchise. She got a salary, and in exchange, she followed rules. This many matches per week. This many dates per month for each client. This many new clients. Numbers were the point, regardless of whether the matches made sense or the dates were meaningful or the clients were admirable human beings.

She'd followed the rules at first, but after a year, she'd started to see how those regulations made things worse for women who'd been through dating hell. Meaningless dates translated to more rejections. Bad matches led to more breakups. Elisa did better—meaning she made more women happier—when she followed her own guidelines, setting up dates only between people she genuinely believed would like each other and pushing for ongoing contact only for couples she truly thought had a future. The number of solid-looking marriages that came from her work—the only measure that mattered to her—was better than anyone else's in the company.

Maybe the franchise owner was jealous of Elisa's success, or maybe she'd just drunk way too much Kool-Aid, but for whatever reason, she cracked down on Elisa with full force, putting her on notice. The owner told her that she had to make her quota in the last ten days of the month. There was no way Elisa could do that without sacrificing her clients' happiness, and she told her boss so.

Her boss fired her without notice. Elisa left the office with only her contact list—partly because no one had told her that she couldn't take it with her, but mostly because she would have died before she'd leave her clients hanging. She planned to call every one of them to let them know she'd left and to apologize for having to abandon them while they were still single.

Only it hadn't worked out that way. Every client she'd called had begged her to take them with her.

At first she'd laughed. It had seemed like a crazy joke. Of course she couldn't take them with her. She didn't have a job, and there was no way she was going to start making matches out of her living room.

But that's what they wanted. They pleaded with her. They told her that they'd meet with her in a coffee shop, the park, their *own* living rooms, if that was what it took. They said she made them feel good about themselves. She boosted their confidence, offered them control of their destinies.

She convinced them they didn't have to date jerks.

The outpouring of support made her cry, and then it bolstered her. Why couldn't she do it? All she needed were clients, a telephone, an office and maybe—down the line—an assistant. That wasn't so much, really. She'd taken out a loan to get the office space, set up a business and gradually transitioned her title from "matchmaker" to "dating coach," bringing in new clients and adding services. Evening and weekend workshops and classes. Boot camp outings. Boot camp weekends.

Things were looking good, but she dreamed of offering her services to a wider audience, of evangelizing the notion of hiring a dating coach. If she could grow demand, if she could increase her own reach....

Six months ago she'd been grateful to still have clients. Now she wanted more.

She'd confessed her ambitions to Julie, who'd been incredibly supportive. "Not more, *bigger*. Celebrities. Because if you do that, the idea of hiring a dating coach enters the popular consciousness. And if you're the dating coach that all the big names have, you're the person everyone wants. They know, if you're good enough for Mila Kunis, you're good enough for them."

"But how do you get into that market? You have to have a celebrity to get the celebrities, right?"

Julie had puzzled over that for a minute, then said, "I know someone who knows Celine Carr's publicist."

And two days later, Haven had returned her call.

"Celine's not easy," Haven had said. "And she's made more of a mess of dating than just about any other aspect of her life."

Elisa doubted that, because she knew Celine's brief stint in rehab had been followed not a year later by a term in an eating disorder clinic, or so the tabloids and entertainment magazines had said. But maybe that wasn't true. Look at how news was born—by crazed, aggressive paparazzi. It was a wonder anything factual ever got printed.

"We've got image consultants, we have all that stuff going on," Haven said. "You can focus completely on the dating stuff. I've heard great things about you. But I'd like to meet you before I make a decision."

Haven had arranged a meeting, and Elisa and Celine had immediately hit it off. Or at least Elisa had been charmed by Celine, and Haven had told Elisa, "You're amazing with her. She listens to you. If anyone can get her to shape up, you're my gal."

Since then, Elisa and Celine had met almost weekly, working on Celine's self-image, talking about what the star wanted from a relationship and discussing strategies for a healthy approach to dating.

Which was why it was a bit of a mystery to Elisa why Celine was still picking up strange men in drugstores. Elisa would have to address that one with Celine later tonight.

Elisa had aimed for nonchalance when she'd told Brett about her phone conversation with Haven this afternoon, but it had been a little tenser than Elisa had let on. Haven had been pretty riled up when she'd heard about the paparazzo on the plane. She'd been torn between staying with her mom in the hospital and flying to St. Barts to check out the situation for herself. Elisa had reassured Haven a million times that the situation was under control, but Haven kept saying, "You don't know Celine." Finally Haven had said she'd take a look at what, if any, photos or other material had made it online and would decide based on that whether she thought Elisa needed reinforcements.

Elisa would have to make sure that everything else went smoothly from this point on. When Brett and Celine were done, Celine's evening with Elisa would start. If Elisa and Celine wanted to make the most of the setting, and generate useful promo footage, they probably wouldn't go to bed 'til 2:00 a.m. or later.

What an exhausting thought. Julie had been right when she'd said Elisa had a long evening ahead of her.

She let her eyes fall closed. She'd have a cat nap. Just enough to take the edge off.

But she was restless, and she knew why. Brett. He'd had on a T-shirt at the pool, but it had cleaved to his shoulders and chest. And under his board shorts, his hips had been narrow, his legs gorgeously muscled.

Thou shalt not covet thy client's date.

Oh, but she did. She coveted. When he'd stood over her on the plane, at the pool, she'd been reminded of his size and strength. Of the way he'd overwhelmed her that night on her couch. Stolen her breath out of her body.

You can't have him. Even if he weren't Celine's date, even if this wasn't a gigantic mess, you can't have him. He doesn't want to be had.

Her libido didn't care. It just remembered the rush of pleasure she'd felt when Brett had kissed her. The surge of liquid heat, the slickness between her legs, the way the craving expressed itself in her fingers and toes and eyelashes and freckles.

Her breathing quickened, and casually, as if she might fool herself into thinking she hadn't done it on purpose, she eased her hand between her legs, over her nightgown and panties. She could feel her heat through the layers. The fabric dispersed the vibrations, the tease more provocative than a sterner touch.

A knock at the door startled her.

"Go away," she whispered.

Her mind raced. It couldn't be Celine or Brett. Maybe

it was someone from the hotel, checking to make sure she had everything she needed. Or her videographer. Or a reporter. In any case, she had to get up. She dragged herself off the bed and peeked through the peephole.

It *was* Brett. Without Celine. And he looked worried. That was not good. She couldn't remember ever having seen Brett look worried before.

She swung open the door, then remembered she was wearing her nightgown. She felt exposed, standing there in the doorway, her nipples taut under the thin fabric. She was hyperaware of what she'd been up to only moments before, of the wet heat that had gathered between her legs, of her own shame and excitement. His gaze dropped to her breasts, just for a second. She should excuse herself, run to the bathroom, and put on a bra and a T-shirt. Despite her concern about Celine, she suddenly wished for a reason to linger here, under his gaze.

Wanting that pissed her off. She knew exactly how little that gaze of his meant, and she still craved it. Him. She wanted him to look at her breasts again, and she wanted to slam the door in his face, in equal measures.

She forced herself back to the moment. "Where's Celine?"

"She's doing karaoke with the paparazzo from the plane. Steve. Steve Flynn. He introduced himself and asked if she wanted to get up there with him. I tried to intervene, but short of physical restraint, there was no way."

Elisa's heart sank. "Oh, *shit*."

Brett nodded. "And she's pretty drunk."

"You left her alone?"

"I didn't know what else to do. I left my cell in my room, and she wasn't interested in listening to me. It was faster to just come here than to go back to my room and call you. I figure she'll listen to you."

Elisa's mind ran rapidly over the contours of the scenario. "Morrow is down there?"

He looked at her blankly.

"Videographer," she explained. "Short, bald, speaks in very short sentences, and last seen in a heinous aqua polo shirt?"

"Yeah."

"Filming?"

"I think so. Where'd you find him? Nice guy, but not chatty."

She laughed, despite her worry. "He came highly recommended from a bunch of people, and I loved his work. He's the best freelance videographer for promo in New York. Were there other photographers down there?"

"That blond woman. And there was another guy with a camera—didn't recognize him."

"Crap. We'd better get back down there." She was about to follow him out of her hotel room when she remembered what she was wearing. "Let me go change."

He caught her wrist in one hand. "I don't know. You look pretty great in that."

Maybe it was all the adrenaline already surging through her body, maybe it was the smell of ocean air and sound of surf, or maybe it was the echo of her fingertips brushing over her swollen sex through her clothes, but his compliment sent a rush of heat into the pit of her belly. A matching flush warmed her cheeks. What was he doing?

"Please don't play games right now."

He broke eye contact, his gaze finding a point on the floor.

Did he really think she'd let an empty compliment soften her up? Probably. After all, he was done with Celine. He was ready for his next conquest.

She left him at the door, grabbed a bra and T-shirt and shorts, and went into the bathroom to change. Her face was hot, and her hands shook. It sucked that he still affected her like this. All he'd said was "You look great." Imagine how thoroughly she'd go to pieces if he kissed her.

No, no—don't imagine that. Very bad idea. And yet her body was obviously not interested in cooperating with the master plan, because she could imagine it vividly— Brett pressing her up against the door frame, sliding a thick thigh between her legs, pressing hard muscle—or something even better—against her. She shook her head rapidly, whipped off the nightgown and struggled into her clothes, trying to distract herself from the images.

When she emerged from the bathroom, he was standing inside the door, looking ill at ease. "I didn't mean to make you uncomfortable."

"You didn't make me uncomfortable."

She couldn't read his expression. Busted ego, she hoped.

"We should get down there before she starts dancing on the tables."

He raised his eyebrows. "Would she do that?"

"She does have a history. Dancing on tables, getting publicly dumped, drinking too much and being escorted home by the cops, shaving her boyfriend's initials into her pubic hair and flashing reporters."

He rolled his eyes.

"If you have so much scorn for her, why did you accept the invitation?" She gave him a little shove toward the door.

He held it open and then let it swing shut behind her. "I don't know."

"Just because she asked?" She hadn't meant to push, but the question had come out.

He frowned. They were nearing the elevator. "You don't think much of me, do you?"

"If you were my client, I'd say you don't think much of yourself. That's what I say when women date anyone who expresses any interest in them. But I guess with guys it's different, right? Sowing oats and all that. Wouldn't want your genes to miss an opportunity. Sociobiologically speaking."

"If you say so. You're the expert."

She didn't feel like much of an expert, not around him. She felt in over her head. Drowning. He was walking fast now, giving her an eyeful of his tight butt under faded jeans, the bunch and release of hard male muscle. She followed him into the waiting elevator and instantly regretted it. Stairs would have been so much better. This was a small space, and he was a big presence, and she didn't want to think about whether, if she cornered him, a camera would record their doings.

She couldn't look at him. She counted the pings as they descended and practically leaped out when the doors opened.

Neither of them spoke on the path to the bar. As they approached, they could hear music coming from inside.

"Oh, no," Brett said. "Duet."

The sounds of a twangy, popified guitar, a steady drum machine beat and two voices reached their ears.

YOU'RE MY BEST WORST
    Best worst, best worst
    Friend.

And I knew there was
Only one way this could
End.

"Is that them?" Elisa asked, simultaneously horrified and impressed. She'd heard the song before—she tried to stay up-to-date on pop music, especially romantic pop music—and Celine was doing a really credible imitation of the female artist. Even more impressive, Steve could pull off a kick-ass male accompaniment.

They stepped into the lounge and stopped to let their senses adjust to the overstimulation. A thick knot of people clustered around the bar, and Celine and Steve stood on top of it, arm in arm. They gazed into each other's eyes and belted out the song into a single handheld microphone. In Celine's other hand, she held a peach-colored drink that periodically splashed over the top of the glass and onto the bar.

Absent his hooded sweatshirt, Steve was kind of cute. More like B-grade movie actor than pond-scum paparazzo. He was dark haired and dark-eyed, with a strong, almost aquiline nose and broad shoulders. And star quality to his performance. Neither of them was mailing it in. They were both singing for dear life.

The hoots and cheers only egged them on. Several people held cell phones aloft, capturing photos and videos, and the professionals ripped through memory cards at high speed on the sidelines.

"I thought I was kidding about the tabletop!" Elisa could barely hear her own wail over the music.

At the outside edge of the cluster of groupies, Morrow captured the whole fray on video.

"Oh, God." Elisa held back for a moment, trying to imagine what the coverage would look like. The evening entertainment shows, with their splashy headlines, would proclaim "Celine Carr's romantic weekend implodes in party-girl frenzy!" or something else awful. The photos would be close-ups of Celine's alcohol-dazed face and that drink, tilted at a dangerous angle, in her hand, interspersed with longer shots of her up on the bar.

And who knew what Celine had told Steve, who, it had to be said, looked a lot more goofy than predatory. Celine was just so sweet and trusting. Elisa couldn't let her do this to herself.

"We have to stop her," she said over the interwoven crooning of Celine and Steve.

"How are you going to do that without making it look worse for her?" Brett asked. "If you pull her out now, you'll cause a ruckus. Maybe this isn't such a bad thing? She's just singing, and she sounds good. Maybe this is a bit of fun she's having on her boot camp weekend."

He'd leaned close to talk to her, and she could smell his familiar scent. But worse than all the artificial scents that defined him, she could smell his skin, his Brett essence. And he was close enough that she wanted to put her lips to his cheek and slide them slowly along the roughness of his jaw to his mouth. She wanted to lick his lips, nip them, open herself and invite his tongue in.

Business. Her business. Her reason for being here. Two years ago, his allure had overwhelmed her good sense. But her good sense had been less developed then. She'd been more hotheaded, more of a seize-the-day girl. Now she was a businesswoman on a mission. Rendezvous and its success were more important than the longing between her legs.

Or in her heart.

She shut that thought down and wrenched her wayward brain back to the matter at hand. Maybe he was right about Celine. She could let this song finish, she could cheer along with the rest of the audience, and then she could find a way to drag Celine offstage with a subtler equivalent of a cane in vaudeville.

"Will you help me get her out of here once this song is over? I don't want her talking to that guy. She's not supposed to talk to anyone from the press without supervision."

Brett nodded, then put his hand on her arm the way he had on the plane, and she controlled a shiver. "This is really important to you, huh? This weekend?"

It *had* been really important to her. Now all she wanted was to get Celine off this island and home before someone made a mockery of her in the media or before Celine found a way to ensure a permanent place in the celebrity halls of shame.

"Let's just get her out of here."

"And then later will you tell me why it's such a big deal to you?"

She glared at him. No. She didn't want to tell him anything. But she missed the way she had once told him everything, sitting beside him on his shabby sofa, dining across from him in her impossibly tiny eat-in apartment kitchen, riding shoulder to shoulder on the subway, while she hated herself for bathing blissfully in his warmth.

The song was ending, the final synth notes falling away.

There was a collective gasp from the crowd, followed by a yelp of what could only be pain.

"Oh, shit," said Brett. He dashed into the crowd.

The actress had disappeared from the impromptu stage, and in a moment it became clear to Elisa what had happened. Celine had fallen off the bar.

7

EVERYTHING HAPPENED FAST after that. Elisa leaped into action, barking commands. "Everyone back. Give her some room. No photos." She said it so forcefully that several cell phones snapped shut. Haven would be proud.

Oh, God, *Haven*.

Celine was on the floor, wedged between two barstools, clutching her ankle.

Elisa squatted next to her. "Hon? You okay?"

Celine gave her an imploring look. "It *hurts*."

That wasn't good. "How much? Where exactly?" She leaned closer. Celine smelled like a distillery, and she was bleary eyed. No wonder she'd fallen. Elisa probed the injured ankle gently, and Celine gasped. Really not good.

"We need to get a doctor to look at this. Do you think it could be broken?"

"Hurts," Celine repeated.

"Is she okay?"

Elisa looked up to find Steve hovering over them. "This situation doesn't need its own personal paparazzo," she snapped.

"I'd like to help."

She stood so she could address him face-to-face. "I think we saw enough of your brand of 'help' on the airplane."

"Hey—I'm sorry about that. I was doing my job, but—okay, here's the thing. I'll back off." He put his hands up, a gesture of surrender. "Celine and I were having a good time. I like her. I'm putting the camera away. Okay? No more photos."

"You shouldn't be here."

"I want Steve to stay." The slushiness of Celine's sibilants said she was even drunker than she looked and smelled. "He's nice. Nice to me."

Was Celine naive? Too drunk to be able to think through consequences?

"It's not a good idea."

"That's not your decision, though, is it?" Steve's dark eyes bored into Elisa.

"This is none of *your* business. I asked you to leave."

"Someone's gotta look out for Celine." Steve cast his gaze critically from her to Brett and back again. "What kind of dating coach poaches her client's date?"

Two hands shot out of nowhere and connected with Steve's chest. He fell back against the bar. Brett stood over him. "Watch what you say, asshole. Unless you want to step outside."

She'd never thought of Brett as physically intimidating before, probably because she'd never seen him threaten someone, but with his jaw set, his fists clenched and muscles rippling under his lightweight sweater, he was all outraged male. She wouldn't want to tangle with him, at least not in a fight.

She wouldn't want to tangle with him, period, she reminded herself. Because she knew exactly what would happen if she did—both the bliss of the moment and the anticlimax that would follow. Even if his shoulders and back and arms were magnificent and she couldn't look away. He'd just physically assaulted someone who'd insulted her. She wasn't supposed to find that attractive, was she? It was so—primitive. And sexy.

"I don't know how you live with yourselves," growled Steve, righting himself and straightening his clothes, like a movie cliché.

Brett stepped forward, but Elisa came to her senses and grabbed his arm. "No. Leave him alone. Do you know anything about ankle injuries?" She squatted again by Celine.

Brett knelt, too, heat pouring off him. He was close enough that his breath brushed the side of her neck, and desire unfurled low in her belly. "Not much. I've had a few sprains." He took the ankle in his hands and checked it over. "The fact that you're not screaming means it's not broken—I know that much. You probably sprained it, Celine." To Elisa, he said, "Do you think we could get her to a doctor?"

"I don't know how easy it'll be to find a doctor on the island," Elisa admitted. She needed to keep her mind on the situation, not on the way that Brett's nearness had started a low thrum of electric heat all over her body.

Around them, people returned to the business of eating dinner. Elisa saw cell phones and cameras waggling again. But as much as she wanted to grab them out of people's hands, drama would only make things worse.

Steve now knelt beside Celine. They smiled at each other.

It was like Stockholm syndrome. Celine was going to serve this guy her life story on a silver tray in a few minutes. Elisa had to hand it to him—he was smooth.

"You need to leave. Or I'll call hotel security."

"I just want to help."

"Look, assho—"

She silenced Brett with a look. A brawl would attract more attention. So would bringing in hotel security. The best thing she could do was prevent further confrontations between Brett and Steve. "Okay, fine. Can you go find the resort manager and ask where to find a doctor?"

Steve hesitated, as if calculating whether this was another way to get rid of him.

Celine gave a little whimper of pain, and that seemed to make his decision. He took off for the hotel lobby.

"I wanted him here," Celine pouted. "*He* actually cares."

"Oh, hon, I care."

"You only care about your business. You and Haven only care about how much money you can make off me."

"That's not true." She felt a pang of guilt, though. As much as she'd tried to keep her mind on Celine, she'd been distracted all day with ambition for Rendezvous and inappropriate thoughts about the man standing beside her. She couldn't blame Celine for feeling the way she did. "I do care—both about your ankle and finding you someone special to be with."

Celine gave her a jaundiced look and held her injured ankle gingerly.

Elisa tried not to let it bother her. Celine was in pain, drunk and exhausted. In the morning, things would look better for both of them.

"Can you help me get her back to her room?" Elisa asked Brett. "I'd feel a lot more comfortable if we were all out of the limelight."

Between the two of them, they hoisted Celine up and draped one of her arms over each of their shoulders. She was dead weight and uncooperative, and they more or less dragged her out of the restaurant, across the brick patio and up a small half flight of stairs. Elisa had a moment of gratitude that the star's slim body separated Elisa from Brett, but she was still very aware of him on the other side, his strength, the ease with which he bore most of Celine's weight.

"There's a long flight of really narrow stairs leading up to her room," Brett said.

"Shit." This was too hard. This whole weekend, this whole project, had gone wrong at every turn. Maybe it was time to admit that it wasn't meant to be. She was supposed to have a small, modest business teaching editorial assistants and bank tellers how to date.

No. She hadn't come this far to give up. Even if she didn't owe this to herself, she owed it to all the women who'd helped her build Rendezvous from the ground up. She wouldn't give up on this opportunity now.

She took a deep breath, steeling herself.

"I think it might be better if we put her in your room…?" Brett began.

"Yeah." She tried not to think about the big bed she'd been looking forward to sprawling across.

"I don't want to be in your room."

Elisa hadn't even been sure Celine was conscious until she spoke.

"Tough luck," said Brett.

Not the diplomat, but Celine was quiet, and Elisa was grateful.

They took the elevator to Elisa's floor. By the time they unloaded her onto Elisa's bed and propped her up on the pillows, Elisa was drenched in sweat and panting. Celine had done as little as possible to aid with the transport.

Elisa called the front desk to check on Steve's progress. A doctor was on the way, a woman with a lilting Caribbean accent told her. Elisa gave her the new room number.

A few minutes later, there was a knock on the door. Brett went to look through the peephole, then groaned. "It's him."

"Let him in," Celine demanded.

"Can I have a word with you?" Elisa whispered to Brett.

He stepped too close, and she had to move back to give herself room to think. "Can you convince Steve that he should leave Celine alone? Bribe him or something?"

Brett frowned, and Elisa had to wonder why he was just as hot when he was frowning as when he was smiling. Maybe it was all the little rugged lines on his face. "I really don't think that's a good idea. Bribes only work in movies."

"It's worth a try, though, right?"

"Is it really necessary? He doesn't seem that bad to me. He seems to *like* her. Isn't that what you want?"

"He doesn't seem that bad to you," she repeated incredulously. "You smashed his memory card on the plane and shoved him just now. What do you do to guys you don't like?"

Something like embarrassment crossed Brett's face. "Yeah, well, that's different from buying him off. She *likes* the guy. You heard her. You have to give her a little more credit. What's the worst thing that can happen?"

"He could destroy her in the press and break her heart."

"Man, you have a dark mind. You seriously think that's going to happen?"

"Brett." She put her hand on his forearm where his sweater was rolled up, then pulled away. The dusting of curly hair over his warm skin and the cords of muscle were too distracting. She had to talk quickly because Celine was pulling herself upright, apparently prepared to limp all the way to the door. In her drunken state she was going to hurt herself worse. "This guy is very clever and sneaky. I mean, what the hell was he doing, singing karaoke with Celine in the first place? He's got some kind of plan, and Celine's going to get hurt."

Celine teetered between the bed and the door.

"Please?" Elisa said.

He sighed. "Okay. I'll talk to him."

Brett went to the door while Elisa helped Celine back to bed. She could hear the rise and fall of Brett's and Steve's voices outside, spiking in anger.

"You'll be fine. Back on the horse by tomorrow," Elisa told Celine, partly to cover the sounds of the argument in the hallway and partly to reassure herself.

"I can't do dating boot camp with a sprained ankle."

Elisa was inclined to agree, but at the moment she couldn't let herself think about that. "You don't know it's sprained. Tomorrow we can go into town—the bakeries are supposed to be amazing—get you some coffee and plant you by yourself at a little table by the window, maybe? Easier on the ankle than hiking or shopping. And a great way to meet a man and get to know him." *Sober and with your clothes on.*

"I met a man. Brett. You screwed it up. Then I met another man, and you screwed that up, too."

All traces of the sunny TV star had vanished. Maybe it was the pain, maybe it was the drunkenness, or maybe

Celine Carr had just had enough and no longer wanted
to play the game. Elisa couldn't blame her. If Elisa
wasn't supposed to be the grown-up in this situation,
she'd be bawling by now.

Brett came into the room without Steve, gave Elisa
a tight nod of affirmation and said to Celine, "He said
to tell you he's sorry about what happened, and he'll
see you around."

Celine frowned. "What did you say to him?"

"I pointed out to him that if he really had your best
interests at heart, he'd see that he probably wasn't going
to help your situation here by hanging around."

"What'd he say?"

"He said I was right."

Celine's shoulders slumped, causing Elisa a pang of
sympathy. What a miserable day the actress had had.
One rejection after another. This was nothing like the
weekend of being adored that Elisa had promised her.
"Tomorrow, I swear, we'll get you back out there and
help you to enjoy this weekend."

"I was enjoying this weekend. With Steve."

Elisa was about to answer her, but Brett put his hand
on Celine's arm. "For what it's worth—Steve said he
had a good time with you."

That seemed to settle Celine down. She rested her
head back on the pillow, and if she didn't exactly smile,
some of the hurt and worry smoothed out of her forehead. "He used to be a fine arts photographer, and he
had a gallery representing him, but it burned down. He
couldn't make enough money to stay in New York, so he
started taking celebrity photos. He hates it, though. He
wants to go back to taking the photos he wants to take."

*Which he'll be a lot closer to doing after he makes
a killing spreading photos of you all over the web, the*

weeklies and the evening entertainment shows, thought Elisa.

"He sounds like an interesting guy," said Brett. "If you weren't a celebrity, and he weren't a paparazzo, you guys could have a good time. But Elisa's right. No point in setting yourself up to get used and abused."

Celine rose partway from the pillow, protest already on her lips, but Brett plowed on. "And, hey, I meant to say this earlier. Doctor's on his way. There *are* doctors on the island, but we're getting a special visit from a guest who happens to be an orthopedist. Lucky you."

"I just want to go home." Celine sounded more like a six-year-old than a twenty-two-year-old.

Elisa stroked her hair back from her forehead. "The doctor'll be here soon. Rest for now, and if you want to go home, we will tomorrow."

She knew it was weakness, but the thought of going home tomorrow filled Elisa with a profound sense of relief.

8

"WELL, THAT SUCKED."

Brett stepped out on the balcony and stood behind Elisa, who was sipping a glass of wine. The view here was of secluded, quiet water. A string of lanterns disappeared off to the left, leading, he guessed, to the bar's open-air seating area. He thought he could hear laughter and a tinkle of glasses from that general direction, but maybe that was just Caribbean fantasy.

She stared out at the water, face set. "It did, didn't it?"

Celine was asleep inside, her breathing deep and even. The doctor had come, diagnosed a sprained ankle and given her a pain pill that had knocked her out in a matter of minutes. Brett didn't know about Elisa, but he was more than happy to see the outside of Celine's eyelids. The worst part was how bitchy she'd been to Elisa, who was only trying to make the best of a bad situation. She'd been calm and cool under pressure, holding off the photographers and managing Steve. She'd called Haven, a conversation that had consisted of shrill squawking on the other end of the phone and Elisa murmuring reassurances until finally she'd started just say-

ing, "Yes. Yes. Of course. Yes. She's your client. Yes.
If that's what—yes." She'd hung up, expression stormy,
then had gone to Celine's room to retrieve a few of her
things. Upon returning, she helped wrangle the actress
out of her clothes and into her PJs while Brett stayed in
the hall. And all the while, she'd been kind to Celine,
even when Celine was whiny and nasty. He'd wanted
to strangle Celine by the end.

Speaking of wanting to do violence—he'd surprised
himself with his own hotheadedness when Steve had
insulted Elisa. When was the last time he'd shoved a
guy over anything? Probably when he was seventeen.

Something had snapped in him, some protective in-
stinct that, after all these years, Elisa still called up.
They'd been close friends—it was natural to be protective of your friends, even after so much time had passed.

A breeze blew off the ocean and shifted strands of
her auburn hair. If he reached out, he could touch her
hair, run his fingers through it and wrap a hank of it
around his hand. Tilt her head and find her mouth.

His body roared to life at the thought.

"You want a drink?" Elisa asked.

He took another step closer in the now-chilly night
air. Elisa held her glass up, as if for a toast. "Minibar.
Get yourself something?"

"It's going to cost you a fortune."

She shrugged. "This fiasco is going to cost me a fortune."

He went back into the room where Celine slept in
the king-size bed, a small lump in a sea of white. The
minibar had a better selection than his liquor cabinet at
home, including a collection of proper glasses for wine,
champagne, highballs, lowballs and shots. He poured
himself two miniatures of Jack Daniels and turned off

most of the lights in the room, leaving only a small desk lamp lit before returning to the balcony and pulling the glass doors shut behind him. With less light, they could see the ocean spread out below them, the crests of the subdued waves lit by the moon. He was suddenly, un-accountably happy.

"Can I ask you a question?" Her voice was low, her fatigue evident.

"Shoot."

"Why are you still here?"

He laughed. "You made me stay."

"No, seriously."

"Seriously, that is why I am here. Because you told me I couldn't leave. And you *were* really bossy about it."

She was looking at him in a way that made his blood heat up. With curiosity, with warmth. With possibility. "But you didn't have to, you know, stick around through this whole drama with the ankle."

"What kind of dick would have walked out?"

She turned away.

"Are you thinking, 'The dick I thought you were?'"

A snort of laughter burst out of her.

"You were. You were totally thinking that." And he would never have said this out loud, but his pride was wounded. He knew how she felt about his sex life, but beyond that, he'd always figured she respected him. They'd been friends for a long time, and maybe he'd only been one of many to her, but to him, she'd been special.

"Seriously, Brett, thank you. You were really help-ful tonight."

"Least I could do, after I messed up your weekend."

"It wasn't your fault."

Then abruptly, she was crying, her shoulders shaking.

"Elisa—" He wanted to grab her and wrap her up, but he held the impulse at bay, not knowing how she'd take it.

She swiped at her face. Elisa was not a woman who liked to be seen at a weak moment. Or, in fact, to have weak moments at all.

"Kiddo, it's gonna be okay." The pet name slipped easily off his tongue, and he waited for her to bristle.

Instead, she shook her head. "No. It's not."

"Do you want to tell me about it?"

"No. Yes."

He waited, wondering how she managed to look beautiful and remote even as she dissolved.

"I was working at the matchmaking job, the one I got when we were still hanging out. And it was great. I was doing it, Brett! I was really doing it. Making matches. Making *marriages*. And contrary to what you may think, it wasn't all about you."

"I never really thought that."

"I mean, I'm not going to lie. Watching the way you were—it made me realize that someone had to be out there, standing up for women and giving them an alternative to being at the beck and call of guys like you."

Again, that jab. *Guys like him.* "We're not all so bad," he said mildly.

"That's the point. Guys aren't all the same. You don't have to settle. And it works in reverse, too. Men let themselves be jerked around by women, too. The point is, people, when they're dating, feel like the opposite sex holds all the cards, and traditional ideas about dating reinforce that belief. I wanted to take a different perspective. I *did* take a different perspective. 'Give her the right match and she'll make a fire that'll burn for the rest of their lives.'"

He smiled. Trust Elisa to have boiled her matchmaking philosophy down to an aphorism.

"And it was working. I was good."

A light caught his eye near the horizon, a boat, moving across the water. His legs were getting tired from standing, but he didn't want to do anything to break the spell. He wanted to keep her talking all night. "Tell me what you do as a dating coach."

She smiled into the distance, and a strand of hair blew loose. He watched her tuck it back behind the curve of her ear. He wanted to bury his face there and follow her scent down her slim neck and into the hollow of her collarbone. He cut that thought off before it could dive lower, but not before it made his balls tighten.

"It's fun. Really fun. I do self-esteem-building exercises with them, get them to see and play to their strengths, talk to them about what they want in a relationship and how they might be undermining their own goals, dress them up, help with makeup, coach them on body language."

"Body language, like what?"

"I encourage them to be aware of the signals they send. Some language encourages, like touching hair, touching cleavage, licking lips, while other body language discourages, like crossing arms or legs."

He watched her lick her lips, a sheen of wetness that made his own mouth dry. And damn, now he was licking his, and his cock was heavy, headed toward hard.

"I take them out, I watch how they interact, I point out where they might have inadvertently chased someone away by not making eye contact, or where they might have been too eager when playing hard-to-get would have worked better. They're skills—all these things are skills."

"So you're probably the superchamp of dating, right? You spot him, you get him?"

She crossed her arms. "I do fine," she said stiffly.

Or, on the flip side, if she was determined not to be drawn in, she was pretty damn good at broadcasting that, too. Not that the crossed arms deterred him—they only pushed her breasts up. And the slightly sulky expression was more turn-on than repellent. "You were telling me about what happened. You were doing it, making matches, and you were good. Here, sit."

The balcony offered two rattan chairs with cream-colored cushions, and he held one out for her.

"Right." She told him the story of how her loser boss had fired her for being good at what she did.

"That sucks."

"I don't feel sorry for myself."

He laughed. "No, I remember you always had strict rules against that."

"The whole Celine thing—a couple of months ago, Julie and I—"

She shot him a look, seeking confirmation that he remembered who Julie was. He gave a tight nod. As if he could forget.

"We were brainstorming how I could grow the business. And she thought I should try to get someone really well-known to be a client, and she said she knew someone who knew Celine's publicist. I knew who Celine was. I watch her show. Do you?"

He shook his head.

"She's kind of brilliant. Do you know the premise?"

He shook his head again, feeling like a heel. He'd forgotten there was substance to Celine's celebrity, that she wasn't just one of those tabloid types.

"Her character was in a car accident, and she was left a quadriplegic."

"Seriously?"

Elisa folded her legs up under her so she was sitting cross-legged in the big chair's embrace. "Seriously. And she—the character—has been struggling to put her life back together ever since. It makes me cry multiple times per month. Her fiancé left her, and she couldn't do her job any more, but she's seeing someone else now, and she's got a great job, but of course all this bad shit keeps happening to her, or it would have been over after the first season."

"Wow." He didn't know what he'd pictured, but it certainly wasn't anything like that. Maybe something teenybopperish, like Hannah Montana.

Elisa sipped her wine, and he watched her tongue flirt with the rim. Blood headed south so fast he got light-headed. He'd been at least semiaroused since they'd stepped onto the balcony.

"It's a great show. If you'd told me that you had the hots for her because of her acting, I'd totally believe that. She obviously has a lot of depth."

He shrugged. "Despite tonight's performance. Although we can't take her behavior tonight too seriously. I hurt her feelings. God knows why, but she likes me."

Elisa shook her head and rolled her eyes at that, and they both laughed. "So, anyway, that's my story. Not much I can do about it now. Haven—that's Celine's publicist—is flying in tomorrow morning. I think the weekend's a lost cause."

He doubted that. But then, here he was, the champion of second chances. He had to be a crazy optimist. "Why do you say that?"

"She originally didn't come on the trip because her

mom was having her appendix out. And now she's leaving her hospital bed to come rescue me—"

"She's not rescuing you. She's rescuing Celine." And surely, if Haven was worth her salary, she knew her client was a total nut job.

"Same difference, in this situation."

Brett screwed up his face at that, drawing a small smile from Elisa. It was surprisingly sweet. He'd like to get her to smile for real.

"Was she angry?"

"No, not angry, exactly. Not at me, anyway. Stressed out."

"So—there you go. Celine will be better in the morning, you'll get things back on track, and Haven can clean up. By the time she gets here, you'll be making it look easy."

"You think I can get Celine to work with me again? She seemed pretty angry."

"If you can't, I'll talk her into it. For whatever sick reason she seems to listen to me."

She pointed a finger at him. "You're authoritative."

"That's just another word for bossy, right?" He laughed. "I hope you're right. I just got this news anchor job, and I think the network's worried I don't have enough gravitas."

"I saw you on TV once," she said meditatively.

"So you're still living in New York."

"Yeah." She got up from her chair and returned to the railing, turning her back on him.

"You knew I was still in New York?"

"Yeah, I knew."

Why did that bother him so much? He hadn't gone looking for her, either. Of course—he had done his share of chasing after her in the early days after she'd dropped out of his life. Calls, emails, friend requests, texts. All for naught. But she'd seen him on TV, and she hadn't dropped him a line to say, "Nice work."

Of course, maybe she hadn't thought it was.

"You looked good. You had gravitas, all right." She said it to the Caribbean, the words whipped back at him by the breeze.

Or maybe she had.

Ah, what did it matter? They were here now. The past was the past, but this was now, and he wasn't going to screw it up by fuming over a cold shoulder he'd probably deserved.

He got up and leaned on the railing beside her.

The silence stretched out too long. Elisa broke it. "How're your parents?"

"Busy. Busier than ever. My dad still works like a crazy man. I think he likes it that way, because he's turned down a few early-retirement offers. And my mom runs around like mad. I don't know how she's busier than when we were kids, but she is. Volunteering, organizing shit. You know. She asks about you sometimes. She always liked you."

"She only met me once."

"You make an impression."

Elisa shook her head, dismissing that. "So. A news anchor. I thought you wanted to be an investigative journalist. You used to say your goal was the *New York Times,* NPR, something like that."

"You remember."

"Of course I remember."

As far as he was concerned, there was no "of course" about it. She'd dropped off the face of the earth for two years, and he'd assumed she'd cleared all the Brett info from her mental cache.

"Turns out I'm not smart enough for that kind of work. You gotta have a lot of substance to do that stuff. I'm more the glitz guy."

Now she was really frowning at him. "You put yourself down a lot, you know that? 'God knows why, but she likes me.' Then 'For some sick reason, she seems to listen to me.' Followed by 'I'm not smart enough… you gotta have substance.' What's that about?"

This was vintage Elisa, chiming in with the pop psych analysis, making more out of everything than was there. "I was *joking*."

"Uh-huh."

"Give it a rest, Elisa. I'm not your client. You don't have to figure me out."

"If you were my client—"

"I'm *not*."

Thankfully, she left it at that. For a moment they sipped their drinks in silence. The scent of the ocean and the resort's floral plantings drifted to them. Overhead, the sky was silly with stars, a dizzying firmament. His brief anger had left him aroused and impatient, and if they had been any two other people on the planet, with any other history, on any other day, he would have followed his dark craving to its logical conclusion, would have turned to her and kissed her. Hard. But he couldn't do that. She'd slap him across the face.

And he'd deserve it. Not only because of what he'd done—*and* hadn't done—two years ago, but because, intentionally or not, he'd landed like a combat boot on her carefully laid weekend plans. On her ambitions.

He tipped back his glass, swallowing a long pull of whiskey. He wanted to reach for her hand. He wanted to reach for her across the years that were between them, across the mess he'd made of things, and tell her that he would make it all right. He wanted to show her the best way he knew to make it right.

Instead, he said, "All you need to redeem yourself with Haven and the media and the rest of the world is for Celine to find someone else she likes, right? Then she's happy, and you've made a match, and the world will be far more interested in that than in more footage of Celine behaving badly. Falling off a bar isn't really that entertaining anyway."

"You'd think that, right? But just wait. That thing is going to be all over the internet by morning. And footage like that has a longer shelf life than you would ever believe."

"Unless something more interesting happens."

"What's 'more interesting' than a party girl relapsing, ending up with the wrong man and falling off a bar drunk?"

"Love at first sight?"

She laughed, a hard, bitter sound. "You don't believe in love at all, let alone love at first sight."

Why did that hurt? He *didn't* believe in love—not her kind, anyway, not arrows through the heart, and chocolates and roses, and happily ever after. "I don't have to believe in it. But I can still help you direct a movie that portrays it."

She frowned at him. "Don't be ridiculous. You're not helping me with anything. You need to get yourself on the next flight out of here."

He didn't want to leave. A few hours ago, he might have told himself that it was because they were friends again, or on their way to being, that he was lured by the simple promise of having Elisa back in his life on the old terms. But now he knew it wasn't true. The moonlight and her vulnerability made a potent combination.

He had to control his hands and talk his body down as he tried his damnedest not to lean over and capture her mouth, twine his fingers into her thick, shiny hair.

God, he wanted to kiss her. He wanted to kiss her so she'd forget she'd ever been kissed before. He wanted to mold her body along the whole length of his, press all the hungry, stupidly lustful parts of himself against her. He wanted to drown the craving. Oh, he was going to lose his mind thinking about it—drown *in* the craving. He could make her forget all about Celine Carr and the media and the rest of the world.

Selfish bastard. She was trying to save what mattered to her, and all he could think about was his cock. He hadn't deserved her friendship before, and he didn't now.

She was watching him. Watching him watch her, her eyes big. And then her gaze slipped, just for a moment, to his mouth.

He didn't think; he just pounced.

SHE'D KNOWN HE was going to kiss her before it happened, and still, it was a shock. The heat and possessiveness of his mouth, and the way her hands reached for him against her better judgment.

His mouth was so soft, so demanding, so *giving*. It made her cells sing with pleasure. And were those her fingers in his hair? And her other hand on his back, clutching him, noting the shift and bunch of the muscles there?

She was aware of her body, like a chant. *Want. More.*

His tongue urged her lips to open, and she let him in. The stroke of his tongue against all the tender bits of her mouth made her sigh. He groaned in response. That sound undid all her resistance, and she pulled his head down to get more of him. He tasted so good, of whiskey and wine and Brett. She knew this kiss, knew it inside and out, knew that he was going to bite her lower lip before he did, knew that he wanted her to meet his thrusts and that, when she did, she'd feel it down to her toes, that slide and urgency.

Want. More.

She did. She wanted him to pick her up and carry her into the room where—

Where Celine was sleeping.

Reason rushed in like an unwanted rainstorm. This *could not happen.*

She let go of his head and gently shoved his shoulder.

He looked back at her with lust-glazed eyes.

"Are you *crazy?*" she demanded. Of course what she meant was, *Am I crazy?* Which clearly she was. "This situation isn't screwed up enough as it is? What if there's some stealth paparazzo with a night lens out there?"

"Shhhh," he said, extending his hand.

She dodged it. "Don't do that again. Ever."

"Oh, but I want to do it again."

"No. Never gonna happen."

"I want to do it again, and I want to do it for longer next time, and I want you to squeak like that again."

"I didn't squeak." She hadn't, had she? She tried to think and remembered the rush of wet heat she'd felt when he'd bitten her. Maybe then. Her body had a mind of its own, and it was dazed with years-old lust.

"You did," he confirmed. "And, God, you can kiss. Let's do that again."

He reached for her, and she wanted to just give up everything and fall into him, so she did the next best thing, which was to become furious.

"Stop it. No. I'm wise to your M.O. and *no*. No way I'm going to be your next victim."

He drew back. "I don't have victims." He was angry. "Jesus, Lise, you're harsh."

"Conquests, then. You have conquests. You're done with Celine, and you're ready for the next fix, and I'm conveniently available. Well, that's not gonna happen. I'm not going to be your next twenty-four-hour entertainment."

"Twenty-four-hour—"

"Have you ever thought about it? Really thought about it? That's how long it is, Brett. Twenty-four hours, and then you're done. Ready to move on. Next conquest."

"They're not conquests! They're partners! I have partners. They're willing, Lise. Celine was willing. Your sister was *willing*."

How dare he? How dare he bring up Julie? "That's not the *point*. I know they're willing. They don't know any better!"

"They're willing because they're attracted to me and because I make them feel good. Like I was making you feel good. Tell me that's not true." He pointed a finger in her direction, then shook his head and dropped his hand. "No, don't even. I don't need you to tell me. I heard you. I felt you. I *smelled you*."

If she hadn't been so angry, she would have whimpered.

"So that's why women sleep with me. Not because I use magic on them or trick them or lie to them. Because they *want* to. So just shut up about the conquest thing."

But she couldn't. Because if she shut up now, he would kiss her again, and she would let him, and one way or another they would find a horizontal surface, and she would be one—conquest or victim or part-ner—for twenty-four hours. And she couldn't do it. She couldn't risk Rendezvous. She couldn't risk—

"You believe whatever you want, Brett. Whatever lets you sleep at night. But I don't want anything to do with your games. I didn't then, and I don't now."

"Understood," he said tightly.

She had to give him credit. If she'd been in his shoes, she would have had to make some pride-saving final shot, some stab about how the kiss hadn't meant that much, anyway. But he just picked up his whiskey glass and carried it into the room. She heard the water run in the bathroom—he was rinsing out the glass. He'd always been a nice boy that way—good manners, careful with her stuff, helpful when he was in her apartment. He'd been a good friend, and the truth was, her anger was already cooling enough that she knew he didn't deserve the things she'd said to him. No matter who he was. No matter what had happened two years ago.

He set the glass on the desk without looking at her and let himself out.

She had the overwhelming feeling she'd been here before.

The last time she'd felt Brett's mouth against hers, the last time her reason had been overwhelmed by the smell and taste of him, they'd been out beforehand at a see-and-be-seen bar called Aquarium. Aquarium was set up to look like the inside of a fish tank, with win-dows and blue light and projections of moving ocean. They had gotten very drunk, sung on the subway and stumbled up the steps to her apartment, where they'd collapsed together on the couch. She felt like she was still in a fish tank as the world swayed gently all around her, and Brett's face was very close to hers, swaying a

little also, and getting closer? Or was she so drunk she
only thought that?—No, definitely getting closer, and
her heart started to pound, and her mouth went dry,
and her hands shook. She could feel the warmth of his
breath move across her face like a spring breeze, clean
and slightly alcoholic.

The kiss, when it came, was a revelation. A moment
of sweet and then hours, years, of hot, the unfolding feel
of him letting go, pouring himself into her. His hands
were in her hair, clutching her, then on her arms, her
waist, her hips, drawing her closer. Fingers tugged her
shirt from her jeans, and she heard her own moans and
his grunts, each sound pulling something deeper from
inside her, relief and yearning and a desire to laugh and
hold on to him forever.

She felt his hands on her bare skin, and her nipples
hardened under the lace cups of her bra, tight knots
that stole her attention from the feathery touch on her
belly and the wet heat gathering at the juncture of her
thighs. The ache made her cup his head and pull him
closer, made her kiss him harder, trying to have more
of his mouth. More of him. All of him.

He slid a warm hand up, and she whimpered when he
cupped her breast and found her nipple with his thumb.
He made an answering choked sound deep in his chest.
She moved her hands from his head to his broad shoulders, then down over his pecs, so hard, so tense—she
could feel the restraint. The fact that he was holding
himself back, because he wanted her that much, did
crazy things to her, and she was on her knees on the
couch, ready to throw a leg over his so she could strad-
dle him and get herself closer.

Then he'd suddenly broken it off and drawn back.
"I'm drunk," he'd said.

And then, the worst: "I'm sorry."

She couldn't speak because all the lovely heat that he'd summoned up in her body had solidified into a chunk of ice around her heart.

"I'll go," he said. He got up off the couch so quickly he'd smacked his leg into the coffee table and hurried toward the door.

Just before he went out, he turned and said it again, so she saw how deeply he meant it. "I'm sorry."

She'd stared at the door for quite some time after he'd closed it, not willing to admit he was gone.

That had been the worst. The having and the losing and then—nothing.

No—that was a lie. That hadn't been the worst. The worst had been two weeks later, when her sister, Julie, had come to visit.

ELISA HAD KNOWN her sister was on the market and raring to go. Julie had made no bones about the fact that she was on the rebound, or that Brett was a potential target. She'd asked Elisa point-blank whether he was available and whether Elisa had dibs.

"Or even if you don't have dibs." Julie had tucked her shiny blond hair behind her ears and scrutinized her sister's face. "Even if you feel like it would be weird for me to sleep with your friend. I won't do it if you think it would be weird."

Weird. Julie had no idea what had happened between Elisa and Brett, because as far as Elisa was concerned, nothing had happened. Certainly Brett was acting that way. A few days after the post-Aquarium kiss, he'd called her, and they'd had a tentative phone conversation in which neither of them had mentioned the kiss. She'd almost started a thousand different sentences.

What was that? Can we do it again? Are we ever going to talk about this? But she'd been too relieved they were talking at all and too afraid of what answer she'd get if she pushed. After a few more days he'd showed up at her apartment with his Scrabble board. During the game she'd made herself breathe through her mouth so his scent would not be a constant temptation, all the while refraining from looking at his lips. And things were almost normal, even if her own laughter felt tight.

She'd become an expert over those next two weeks in rolling on past the twinge in her chest. She repeated to herself what she'd always known: that there was no future, not even a tomorrow, in Brett Jordan.

So there was no way she was going to tell Julie the truth or admit how foolish and hopeful she'd been in the face of years of evidence. It was better to just allow the incident to slide away into the Aquarium-blue haze from which it had crawled.

"Believe me," said Elisa. "I have the firmest evidence that Brett Jordan is not interested in me."

"But you're interested in him?"

She made a scoffing sound.

"Because I wouldn't want to—"

"No," she said, before her heart could protest. "It's fine. But just so you know," she told Julie, "he's not much for relationships. He's more the one-night-stand type. Forewarned is forearmed."

Julie had laughed and said, "*Rebound.* One night is perfect. And he's not my type, anyway. Too surface."

"Jules?"

"Yeah?"

"I—don't take this the wrong way. I don't want to hear about it. Afterward."

Julie had stared at her, long and hard. "I don't have to do this, Lise."

"No. It's fine. Go for it. Just—no details, okay?"

"Deal," Julie said.

So, no, she didn't think Brett had taken advantage of Julie. Julie hadn't been a conquest or a victim—she'd been, as Brett had said, a partner, kind of a partner in crime, in fact. The three of them had gone out for drinks, and Elisa had stayed as long as she could stand it, until the flirtation between Julie and Brett had become unbearable. Then Elisa had left, and Julie had not come home until nearly 4:00 a.m.

Lying awake in the early hours of the morning, Elisa had wanted to stab herself in her mind's eye. She was not someone with a particularly vivid imagination, but she had been able to imagine Julie and Brett together, kissing, whispering, laughing. Brett moving over Julie, his eyes dark with heat.

She knew too much about how it would feel. She had been eaten alive with envy and wracked with frustration, and she had been denied the relief of self-righteousness because she had *given her blessing.*

And yet the ultimate irony had been the rage she'd felt on Julie's behalf when, the very next day, Brett had refused Julie's invitation to get dinner again. Two days later, Julie left New York; and a week after that—during which, Elisa knew, Brett hadn't so much as texted Julie to see if she'd made it home alive—he'd stopped by Elisa's apartment with a steaming bag full of Chinese takeout and a copy of *50 First Dates.*

She'd opened the door to see his finely hewn, slightly scruffy face smiling at her over the brown paper bag. Her heart had lurched, same as ever, and suddenly everything he did was intolerable. He leaned down and planted a kiss in the general vicinity of her cheek, and the heat and scent of him filled her like fury. He swept past her into the apartment and set the Chinese dishes on her coffee table, and the familiarity of it grated against her skin. Even the way he stepped into the kitchen for a handful of serving spoons, getting everything ready for her, was unbearable. He wasn't sheepish or contrite, as if nothing whatsoever were wrong. For him, it seemed, the kiss that had rocked her world hadn't happened, and neither had sleeping with her sister.

There she'd been for a week and a half, with her huge out-of-proportion emotions, feeling like a barbell had been dropped on her chest. Fierce twinges of envy and anger had invaded her everyday activities, sneaking up on her when she had a vulnerable moment.

He had cocked his head from the other side of her couch. "You want me to wrap up a moo shu pancake for you?"

She was done with the way he'd treated those women and the way he'd treated Julie.

And she was done with the way he treated her, as the perfect rest stop between assignations. As if she'd always be here. *Mi coffee table es su coffee table; come on in, make yourself at home, but, no, don't worry about me. I don't need more of you than this.*

"I'm done."

She had said it out loud.

He looked over at her, quizzical. "Done with what?"

"With this." She gestured at him, at *them*—but of course, there was no *them*. That was the whole point.

"I can't do this. Be your friend."

He set down the white takeout boxes of pancakes and moo shu and came toward her. "Elisa, what are you *talking* about?"

"I don't think we should be friends."

"Elisa, I was *drunk*."

"It's not *about* that." Because what else could she say? She couldn't beg him to feel about that kiss the way she'd felt about it. She couldn't make him want her with the same ferocity she'd wanted him.

He held up his hands. "Okay. Let's calm down here. I knew you were gonna be mad about the Julie thing."

He moved as if to pat her arm, but she jerked out of his reach. "Don't touch me."

Or I will cry. Or I will tell you everything. Or I will beg you to love me.

She had seen how that story ended, with crying and stupid too-late laments. And long phone conversations with friends who would say, *I don't know why he doesn't love you,* when in fact anyone could have seen the writing on the wall. *He doesn't love you because he's a commitment-phobic* asshole.

"Lise, come on." His forehead was all wrinkled-up bulldog concern. "If you're mad about Julie, you don't have to be. We—"

"Stop."

"But—"

"I don't want to hear it. I don't want you to talk about Julie. Or anything."

She was seconds, millimeters, away from telling him how little Julie had to do with the way she was feeling. But what would be the point of that? So she could lay her raw feelings bare, and he could very, very gently tell her he didn't feel that way about her, and then their friendship would be over anyway?

"That's not the point," she said. "The point is that you treat women like they're dispensable. And I can't get past that any more."

If he'd gotten mad, the whole mess might have been washed away in the heat of a good, thorough fight. The truth might have come out, the words spilling from her lips, for better or for worse. *I need you. I need more of what we did. I need all of what we could be.*

But he didn't get mad.

He laughed. It wasn't even a real laugh. It was his mellow-guy *Isn't she cute?* chuckle.

"Get out," she said.

"Elisa, come on."

"Just leave."

"Lise. Seriously."

"Get out!"

He backed toward the door, his hands up again. She gathered up the food, shoving it into the bag. She thrust it all toward him, but he wouldn't take it. "It's yours. I brought it for you."

How could one man be so nice and such an asshole at the same time? It was completely mystifying.

"At least take the movie," she demanded. "I don't want to have to return it."

He took it. His eyes were concerned now. "We'll get together soon, when you're feeling better."

Oh, no, no, no, he hadn't just said that. Her feelings weren't a disease.

She flung open the door and pointed into the hallway.

He hesitated a moment before he stepped out. "Call me?"

But of course she hadn't. Nor had she returned his calls or his emails. At first it had been hard. Every one had been a huge internal battle—her craving for his company, her longing to see his smile and hear his banter versus the knowledge that she was doing the right thing for herself. And maybe for him. Maybe, just maybe, he'd see how it wasn't okay, what he'd done to Julie or any of the others.

It had gotten easier over time, but there had still been a terrible moment when she realized the calls and the texts and the emails and the friend requests had stopped. She was surrounded by silence, and in her life was a Brett-shaped hole.

That was the moment she knew it was really and truly over.

9

ELISA DRAGGED HERSELF up through layers of sleep. She had dozed only in fits and spurts, no more than forty-five minutes at a stretch. Her whole body ached from the thin mattress on the rollaway bed the bellhop had delivered last night.

She'd awakened over and over with a confused sense of anticipation and dread. That kiss. Would it happen again? It couldn't. And she had done everything in her power to make sure it couldn't. Yet—

He'd asked her, half in jest, if her dating coach skills meant she was a dating superstar. If only he knew. She'd dated plenty of men in New York, sure. She knew how to get a first date and a second date and a third date. She loved those third dates. The flowers, the romantic dinners, the poetic speeches, the seduction scenes and the thousand little moments of truth that followed: Would his apartment be clean? Would his bed be made? Would he bother with kissing or go as quickly as possible to the main event? She loved the main event.

But relationships?

Two since college. Both under six months in length and none in the past two years.

She knew she couldn't blame Brett Jordan for all of it. She was a big girl and had to own her romantic failures. She was a dating coach, and if she'd been her own client, she would have given herself a big lecture about being too picky. "Lose the list," she'd have said, as she often did to her clients who had pages of criteria for a mate. "You can keep one deal breaker, but that's it." Yet she'd been unwilling to lose her list, hiding behind *smart, well-educated, good earner, at least five-ten.* And that was her problem, hers alone. She also knew—

For almost a decade, she had been waiting for a third date that would merit a fourth. And last night, Brett had kissed her, and she'd known. *That* was what she'd been waiting for. Him. Her deal breaker had always been *not Brett Jordan.*

It was a tug-of-war of emotions. *He wants me, after all.* Then, *I'd have to be crazy to let him touch me again. He's a one-man wrecking machine, and I'm a building that's already been demolished once.*

She dug her face out of the pillow. Sunlight poured around the edges of the drapes, and the big bed was empty, the covers thrown back. She listened for the sound of movement but heard nothing either on the balcony or in the bathroom. She got up and checked both locations, but Celine was nowhere in the room.

She grabbed her phone and texted Celine, then called. It rang and rang before going to voice mail. "I need to know where you are, Celine. Call me as soon as you can." *Don't freak out,* she told herself. *She could be getting breakfast downstairs. She could be sitting at the pool.*

It was almost ten. At five o'clock she had told herself she'd stay on the cot 'til six, then get up and go swim laps. Apparently her exhausted body had had other ideas.

Haven was scheduled to arrive on St. Barts just before noon. Elisa had two hours to find Celine—plenty of time if the actress wanted to be found.

Elisa got up and dressed quickly in khaki capris and a plain pink T-shirt. She hastily pulled her hair back in a ponytail, brushed her teeth, smoothed on lip gloss, frowned at herself in the mirror and went out.

Celine was not in the resort's breakfast room, a big white room with floor-to-ceiling windows. Neither was she tucked into a corner of the bar where some resort patrons were beginning their day early, although Elisa found the bartender from last night, drying glasses with a towel. He was a rough-faced man in his late thirties or early forties with early morning shadow.

"Did you go to sleep last night?" she asked.

He laughed. "Yeah. I just got in a few minutes ago. Bad scheduling. I feel like a wrung-out rag." He demonstrated, then tossed the towel somewhere behind the bar and took out a fresh one.

"Me, too. Hey, you know the girl who fell off the bar last night?"

"Sure. Celine Carr, right? Love her show."

Of course he did.

"Have you seen her? Or, you know, any fuss that would indicate she's been around?"

"Nope." He hung a glass on the rack above his head. "You want me to give her a message if I do?"

"Call Elisa ASAP."

"I can do that. Hey, have you checked out the pool? That's where most people end up when they get lost."

"Thanks," she said.

Elisa's footsteps picked up with her heartbeat, and

she jogged out to the pool. The sun poured down, and the fragrance of flowers was stronger than it had been yesterday afternoon. There were stacks of pristine white towels in rolling carts at both ends of the pool, but no Celine.

You are not her keeper. You are not even her publicist. You're not in charge of her safety.

"No," she muttered to herself, "but my reputation and personal happiness depend on her not doing anything outrageously stupid."

She took out her phone. She should call or text Haven, because maybe—maybe?—Celine had checked in with her. But Haven was on a flight from New York to St. Maarten at the moment. And just in case Elisa managed to locate Celine before Haven landed, maybe it wasn't worth getting Haven all riled up.

She tried Celine one more time. No answer. She left another message.

She made herself walk slowly to Brett's room. She did not want to arrive out of breath and panicked.

She knocked, and he answered right away.

Oh, holy—

It was like taking a body blow—all the air went out of her.

He wore a pair of cut-off black sweats and nothing else. His shoulders were broad, his chest gorgeously defined, his hips narrow, his well-muscled legs covered with brown curls she wanted to brush her hand across.

She raised her eyes and saw that she'd been caught staring. He was grinning, predatory, but she couldn't be his prey. She was here to boot Celine Carr's butt into twenty-first-century-dating shape, and she couldn't let Brett Jordan's physical perfection distract her.

With effort, she fixed her eyes on his face and her

thoughts on the problem she'd come here to solve. "Celine's missing."

He grew serious. "How missing? Missing from the resort?"

"I don't know. She's not eating in the breakfast room or the bar. She's not at the pool. I'm not sure what to do."

"Did you text her?"

She glared. "Yes. And called. She didn't answer."

"Do you guys have a contract? Can you threaten legal action if she doesn't show?"

She frowned. "I guess I *could*. If I thought it would work."

"I didn't know she could get around on that ankle."

"That's what worries me. She must have had some help."

"Steve?"

She nodded. "Haven's going to be here soon. I don't want to have to tell her I lost Celine to a paparazzo."

Unconsciously he rubbed his palm over his chest. She wanted to follow his hand with hers over the contours of his picture-perfect pecs.

But she also wanted him to put a shirt on.

"Can I help look for her?"

"You don't mind?"

He grinned. "I can think of some better ways we could spend the morning. But no, I don't mind."

She couldn't tell if the sexy significance in his words was deliberate. He could have meant they should get some chocolate croissants and sit by the pool. But intentional or not, the suggestion in his voice curled itself around her internal organs.

She took a step back. Another foot of distance wouldn't do anything to staunch the flood of pheromones, but at least it would put her out of scent range.

She guessed he hadn't showered yet, because musk had won out over Pert Plus. Maybe that was her problem. If he smelled like soap and shampoo, generic and clean, she'd be saner. But he smelled like *man* and, worse, like no one but himself.

God, she was lame. A little male sweat and she was done in.

She had to get herself out of here before she shoved him back into the room and followed him down onto the bed.

He surprised her by laying his hand on her cheek. It was warm and strong, and all she wanted at that moment was to turn her head and press her lips into his palm. His fingertips moved lightly, gently, over her skin. "I know I said you could turn this all around today. I believe you can, if that's really what you want. But are you sure it is? To spend your Caribbean weekend chasing after a spoiled superstar who doesn't really want your help? My best friend used to say, 'If you obey all the rules, you miss all the fun.'"

All she could think about was his touch on her cheek and the last thing he'd said. *His best friend.* She shouldn't care, had spent years trying not to care, but she did. All these months, it turned out, what she had truly wanted was for him to find her and tell her that she was too important for him to lose. "Was I? Your best friend?"

His fingers moved into her hair, and his left hand came up to her other cheek. His face was very close to hers. She could see the roughness of his beard shadow, the softness of his mouth. She could feel his breath moving over her face. "You are. You never stopped being."

She was breathless. "I haven't been a very good friend."

"You can make it up to me."

His lips came down on hers. She didn't have time to protest. His mouth was hot and open, no preliminaries. His tongue swept in, owning her, and she grabbed his arms to steady herself, a low moan escaping. He made an answering sound, a growl she could feel like a vibration in his chest.

This was what she had always wanted, all those years when she had sat on his dorm room floor or his apartment couch and listened to the stories of his latest conquests. This was what she still wanted, what she had been trying to protect herself from. She should put a stop to it as soon as possible if she didn't want to find herself broken and washed up on some emotional shore. She pushed against his arms, but feebly. She couldn't stop herself.

Still, he let go, stepping back, dropping his hands from her face.

"You're Celine's date."

He shook his head, obviously frustrated.

"That's why you're here." She didn't let her eyes drop from his face, afraid if she saw that he was hard under those loose shorts, she'd abandon her resolve.

"Elisa—"

"I can't. I'm her *dating coach,* for Pete's sake. And there's a whole history between you and me. I can't forget that."

He rubbed a hand over his face, mussing his hair again. "I'm sorry about your sister. But I want another chance. I want to start over, and I want it to be like this—" He gestured, encompassing them, the kissing, the heat. "And this time I won't do anything dumb like that. Like going out with your sister."

"I'm Celine's dating coach," she repeated, because it

was the safest argument against what she really wanted, the safest way to make herself behave. "And I need to go figure out what the hell she's up to."

His hand made one last pass over his face, rubbing at his temple. "Okay. Let me put on some clothes. I'll help you. But soon—later—I'm going to convince you to give this another shot."

They'd see about that. She had a job to do and ethics to be true to. No promises would make her believe things would be any different this time around.

He closed the door between them, but she couldn't help thinking about what he was doing in there. Letting the soft black sweatshorts drop to the floor. Pulling on underwear—two years ago he'd worn boxer briefs, which she knew because they were draped over every surface of his dorm room and, later, apartment. She wondered if, like some men, he took an extra moment to settle himself in his shorts, a moment she'd always savored when watching her lovers dress. Then he'd pull on slacks and a T-shirt, or maybe shorts and a T-shirt, the T-shirt clinging to the muscles in his torso like a second skin. She was partial to plain tees with a little bit of elastic in the knit.

She had to stop. She was getting turned on thinking about him getting dressed.

It might've been better if he'd decided to be a genuine asshole and push his luck. But he hadn't. He'd listened and snapped into action to help her. She remembered not just that he'd defended her to Steve and to Celine, but all the years in the past when he'd been a good friend to her. Fixing her computer problems and copyediting her résumés, playing *her* wingman in bars, giving her pep talks, shooting hoops with her. It was easy to forget about all the good stuff, especially when she'd made herself walk away, but until the end, until she'd realized that he'd never, ever see her as anyone other than his good bud—he'd done well by her.

He came out. Unfortunately, he was wearing the same black sweatshorts and a heather-gray T-shirt with just enough elastic in the knit to cling to every muscle in the upper half of his body. He must work out. Reporters didn't have enough physical labor in their everyday lives to look that good on their own. She swallowed hard, and said, "Should we split up?"

"Sure. What do you want me to do if I find her?"

"Text me. And stop her if she's doing something crazy."

"You seem to think she's with Steve."

"It's my worst-case scenario," she admitted. "I mean, I know you gave him money, but—"

Brett shook his head. "I didn't give him money."

"What?"

"He refused it. I meant to tell you, but things got so busy."

"But—but—he disappeared."

"It wasn't the money," Brett reiterated. "He said he wasn't going to do anything with his photos yet, but he wouldn't take the money."

"Is that all he said?"

"He said that he just wanted to make sure that Celine got treated right."

She bit her lip. "You think he means it?"

"I do, actually."

She sighed.

"That's completely impossible for you to fathom, huh?" he said. "Why? Because he was obnoxious on the plane?"

"Because he very obviously has an agenda."

"Had an agenda. He had an agenda, but that could have changed. People change."

"No, they don't."

For a moment they stared at each other. His expression was surprisingly fierce, and she looked away.

"Either way, it makes sense for us to check his room before we start combing the whole resort," he said. "Unless you know his cell number?"

She shook her head. She was grateful that he'd said "us." She had no desire to confront Steve on her own.

They went to the front desk first. Elisa didn't think the resort would actually give them Steve's room number, but the woman behind the desk with the lilting accent accepted Elisa's story that Steve was a member of their party.

When they knocked on Steve's door, no one answered, and no sounds came from within, even though Elisa shamelessly pressed her ear to the door for a good minute. She felt a small but solid sense of relief.

"Beach?" he asked.

She shook her head. "I haven't checked there yet. It doesn't seem like a great place to go with a sprained ankle."

"And Celine Carr is a paragon of good judgment."

"When you put it like that…"

10

THEY DESCENDED THE stone steps to the beach. Resort patrons sat under a pavilion nestled at the far end of the beach, sipping drinks and eating breakfast. She surveyed that area, but no Celine. She ran her eyes over the beach, looking for a telltale flash of white-blond hair, but she couldn't locate the petite, buxom, bikini-clad troublemaker. Along the curving shore, she saw red-roofed white buildings and rainbow sails. In the water, people rode Boogie boards and balanced precariously on stand-up paddleboards, and on the sand, a large array of sunbathers greased themselves and rolled to cook evenly, but her scrutiny failed to pick out Celine.

On any other day, under any other circumstances, this would be paradise. The sun shone, and a gentle breeze blew off the stunning green-blue surface of the water. She could smell the salt, the coconut-scented sunscreen, and the faint, perpetual floral perfume of the island.

And the man beside her—any other woman, with any other past, would be licking her lips in anticipation of what he could do to her, sprawling in the sunshine on the beach or back in his hotel room. She wished like hell for a clean slate. If she didn't know how easily he could break her heart, maybe she'd have just let him kiss her until her instincts had overridden her brain. Instead, she was doing the right thing and wishing like hell she wasn't.

Before her sandals touched sand, she spotted Morrow on the beach, coming around the curve from the beach beyond. He saw her and waved.

She hooked her shoes on a finger and trotted over to him, the sand heating the soles of her feet. If she weren't so worried about what Celine was up to, it would have been divine. She would have thrown herself down in the sand and just rested there, the sun warm on her face. Come to think of it, that had been part of what she'd pictured when she'd fantasized about this weekend— sipping tropical drinks on a white-sand beach, gazing at the sea. Snorkeling or scuba diving alongside Celine, watching the younger woman as she flirted with men. Giving her tips about how to keep the ones she wasn't interested in at bay and how to keep the ones she was interested in at arm's length, until the right moment came to narrow the gap. She'd hoped, she now realized, for a working vacation.

"Have you seen her?" she asked as she came within hailing distance of Morrow. He wore garish surfer shorts and a white polo shirt, and he was barefoot. He had hairy hobbit feet, she noted.

"Went that way." He gestured down the beach in the direction he'd come from.

She started off that way.

"At least twenty minutes ahead of you," called Morrow. "Don't think they want company."

She turned back. "They?"

"With the dark-haired guy. Hot and heavy, too."

"What?"

"Making out on the beach. Had quite an audience."

"Dammit!"

Morrow looked amused. She glared at him, and his smile faltered.

She felt Brett's hand come briefly to rest in the small of her back, comforting, steadying, before it moved away again. He'd come up behind her while she was talking to Morrow.

Her phone buzzed in her pocket. She pulled it out. There was a text from Haven.

In St. Maarten, about to board puddle jumper. What's going on there? There are pictures up on that paparazzi photo site, Razzle, of her with that guy.

"Okay," Elisa said. "Okay." The word was meant to comfort herself, to slow her heart, which was jerking around in her chest cavity like a panicked weasel.

Morrow was watching her curiously. "You want me to give her a message if I see her again?"

"You mean Celine?"

He nodded.

"No." She had little faith a message would be heeded.

"That guy. The hoodie guy. What's the deal with him?"

"He's a paparazzo we picked up. Parasitically, not romantically."

"You said an exclusive." His eyebrows drew together in a scowl.

"You have an exclusive," she said. "Celine and I aren't doing interviews with anyone except you."

"He seems awful chummy."

Behind her, Brett laughed, but cut it short without her even having to glare at him.

She didn't have time for the videographer's insecurities. "I said you had an exclusive, and Celine and I won't give interviews to anyone else. You have full access." She had a strong desire to cross her fingers as she said it.

He nodded, but the crease between his brows didn't ease. "She's talking an awful lot to him."

"Talking's not an interview, last I checked." She needed to find Celine. "We can discuss it more later, if you're still worried."

He shook his head and grunted, "Headed back up. Gotta get lunch. Assuming you don't need more footage of those two? Let me know if you do need me. Got my number in there?"

"Somewhere," she managed to say.

He trooped off across the sand.

She buried her face in her hands and felt Brett's palm on her back again, a soothing antidote to the panic brewing in the rest of her body.

"Lise."

"I've got to find her."

She dialed Haven's number. It was hard to hear the phone ringing over the gentle *shhh* of the surf. She put a finger in her ear, but it didn't help, and her beautiful surroundings clung like claustrophobia, mean and close.

"You have reached—"

She hung up on Haven's voice mail. She must already be on the Orville & Wilbur special from St. Maarten to St. Barts.

"What'd she say?"

She showed him the message from Haven.

"What's Razzle?"

"She told me about it last night. There were a few photos up from the karaoke. It's a site where anyone can post celebrity photos. Paparazzi do, and people who aspire to be paparazzi."

"You can aspire to be a paparazzo?"

Despite her tension, she giggled.

"You know this isn't your fault, right?" His voice was gentle, as gentle as she'd ever heard it.

She turned away from him so he wouldn't see the tears.

"C'mere."

He drew her into his arms. She let herself be held, let herself savor how strong he was, how muscular. How the warmth of his body seeped into hers, comforting her. Heating her, until her core responded by glowing with heat of its own. "You did everything you could," he said into her hair, and she could feel his breath move across her scalp, a tease and a balm. "No one could have done better."

She had to pull away before she answered her desire to tilt up her face and find his mouth. She looked away from him, down the beach, not willing to let him see the need she knew was written all over her face.

She didn't want this. She 100 percent didn't need another complication.

"What do we do next?"

She looked down the beach. "She's down there somewhere, right?"

"If Morrow's to be believed." He didn't sound at all certain of that.

She crossed her arms. Something about his embrace had resuscitated her determination. She would *not* go down without a fight.

"So, we wait."

HE SAT IN the sand beside her. It was close to midday now, and the sand was hot, soaking through his shorts. His balls snuck up closer to him to escape the radiance—or maybe that was because Elisa looked so good in her clingy pink T-shirt. He was particularly fond of the contrasts she made, sharp collarbones and maybe a rib or two, and then her breasts, a perfect handful, beckoning. In the sun, her skin glowed and her eyes were a bright, soft brown. Even her feet turned him on, her unpolished toes digging in the sand.

The sun was relentless, so hot he wished for a water bottle, or to strip off his T-shirt. He'd love to see the same look on Elisa's face as when he'd opened the door shirtless. He hadn't done that deliberately, but when her pupils had dilated and her tongue had peeked out to touch her lower lip—well, he'd been glad he'd forgotten.

He liked the way she'd lit up at the sight of him. It made him think she'd be as eager as he'd imagined, tough and feisty and fun. And damn, there went his own reaction again, and he had to talk it down to avoid the tent-in-the-shorts.

For now, though, he just wanted to erase the misery from her face. To make her smile again, any way he could. He wasn't sure when taking care of her had become a mission for him, but he knew he couldn't stand that she held herself responsible for Celine's antics.

He cast about in his brain for a distraction, but all that came to him were memories of her from college, a flood of silly and meaningless moments. He'd done a good job of compartmentalizing those moments during the two years she'd denied him contact, but now they'd all swarmed back. The good, the bad, and—

He laughed out loud. "Do you remember the snowman?"

"Oh, yeah! Whose idea was that?"

That night had been as different from this moment

as it was possible to get. Dark, just a sliver of moon in the sky. Cold, mid-twenties and crisp. Snow was falling, had been on and off all day and most of the week.

Snow had settled on her hair as they'd walked together across the quad. He couldn't remember where they'd been coming from, and it didn't matter. They walked together, and the snow on the ground and the snow in the air filled the world with that secret winter hush, a cushion against sound. A bubble of silence around them.

She'd gestured at an enormous pile of snow where the campus maintenance team had shoveled out the walkways on the quad and heaped all the remains at the side of Fletcher Dorm. "That's a funny pile. If we carved out a little bit there, and then climbed up and piled some more on the top, we could make a giant snowman."

Her nose had been red in the yellow glare of the streetlamp. There were snowflakes in her eyelashes. He had the unlikely thought that he'd remember that exact moment forever.

He had run to the snow pile and begun carving out huge hunks of it with his mittened hands. She joined him, and they made short work of it, patting down the carved-out snow to shape the bottom third of the snowman. When they were done with that, she had climbed up as high as she could, and he had passed snow up to her to make the top part of the snowman.

She patted the side of her creation. "He has a very small head."

"I won't say anything crass."

"Phone the press!" She clambered down.

Sitting here in the white sand, the aquamarine sea sparkling, that whole night now seemed improbable. But it had happened. They had built a gigantic snowman. It had been hot, dirty, exhausting work. Afterward they had lain back and made snow angels, staring up at a black sky smattered with stars, the snow a blanket around them.

He thought, looking around at the scantily clad tourists, soaking up the bright and noise and heat of this beach, that it had been one of the best nights of his life.

She smiled at him, the smile he'd hoped to coax from her. Straight white teeth and soft pink lips and—

That night he had not let himself think that he could kiss her. There were women you slept with, and then there was Elisa. If he slept with her, who would he make snowmen with?

When he had made his big mistake, the night he had finally given in to temptation and settled his mouth on hers, he had felt like the world had been remade. Elisa was his, hot and soft and mobile in his arms, everything he'd ever wanted and been afraid to ask for. But as the heat had risen, one thought surfaced: *this is the end of our friendship.*

That was what had made him run. That was what had made him bury the pleasure and the relief, and pretend it had never happened.

That was what had made him think he could wash the madness away with Julie, which of course hadn't worked. Julie was so much like Elisa, so visually tempting, and even some of her mannerisms were the same. But early in the morning of their date, midway through their second B-grade horror movie, when he'd tried for the third time to get Julie to provide color commentary with him, and she'd shushed him, he'd felt so tired. Too tired. Shortly after that, they'd kissed good-night, a kiss that was brief and desultory. And he'd sent her home to her sister, not understanding. Where had it gone, all the attraction he'd felt for her earlier that week, earlier that day, earlier that evening? Could it just *vanish* like that? And why wouldn't his attraction for Elisa do that?

That attraction still hadn't diminished.

She was smiling as she remembered that snowy night. "Your mittens were the eyes, and my gloves were the nose and mouth."

"Did you ever get yours back?"

"Never. But it was worth it.

They grinned giddily at each other. Sand, water and blue sky made a dizzying background that contrasted with her reddish hair, and if they hadn't been in public and things hadn't been so screwed up, he would have kissed her just the way he should have that night in the snow. Maybe he would anyway—

Only she frowned suddenly. "I don't think they're coming back this way. What's down there?"

She crawled a few feet over to where two women sunbathed beside them. "Excuse me," she said. "If someone goes down the beach that way, is there another way up?"

"Sure." The woman was clad in a red bikini, her skin an alarming wrinkled brown. "There's another flight of stairs a ways down. And if you walk around the point, there are more resorts and more stairs."

Elisa jumped, then clapped her hand to the pocket of her capris and tugged out her vibrating phone. She looked at the screen and said, "Oh, shit. Haven's here."

She held out the phone, and Brett looked.

It was a fuzzy photo, but against a background of Caribbean blues and whites dotted with sailboats and red roofs, there was no mistaking Celine and Steve, lips locked.

11

ELISA TOLD BRETT he didn't have to come with her, but he followed her from the beach back to the main resort lobby. The lobby was simple and beautiful—white walls, white-tiled floor, white columns holding up arches. Along the walls there were mirrors and windows and dark wood tables and benches, one of which Brett now lounged on, the picture of patient and casual. Her heart gave a little twinge, and she told it to shut up.

Haven stood beside a tall white planter overflowing with green and pink foliage, matched in intensity only by her hot-pink patent-leather wheeled carry-on. The petite PR genius was balanced precariously on high-heeled sandals on the lobby tile, resplendent in skinny jeans, a tight black top and an unholy amount of makeup, her dark hair long and glossy. Elisa hadn't registered her as quite so intimidating the first few times they'd met. But of course, Haven hadn't had reason to be bullshit angry at her before.

The first thing Elisa said was, "I'm so, so sorry." She braced herself for the worst.

But Haven only smiled, her severe face softening. "Sweetie. You cannot beat yourself up about this."

"You had to fly here."

"I chose to fly here."

"Your mom is sick."

Haven smiled wryly. "When you work for Celine Carr, no one's allowed to get sick."

"I—"

"I should have known better than to throw you in the deep end like this. Celine's tough enough to manage under controlled circumstances. I'm just sorry this has turned out this way. I know you were hoping—I was hoping, too. For your sake, but of course for mine, as well."

It sounded an awful lot like an ending to Elisa. "We could find her. It's only midday Saturday. We have two more days. We could—" She wanted, still, to redeem herself. She wasn't ready to believe that Celine's impetuous dating style was incurable.

"Sweetie," said Haven kindly. So kindly it made tears gather behind Elisa's eyes again. "Sometimes you just have to cut your losses with Celine. She texted me this morning to say she wants to call off the weekend because she's met the man of her dreams. She says she's in love with this guy, Steve."

"She's known him twenty-four hours."

"We both know Celine isn't in love with this guy. Who, by the way, is not a very nice guy. He has a history of exposing celebrities this way, by publicizing their locations on the web. There was one situation where a celeb was sexually assaulted by a fan who got her location off one of those sites—from one of his photos—and when he was called out on it, he was pretty unrepentant."

"Crap. Are those his photos on Razzle?"

"I don't know. The username is Tomorrowsnews." Haven hoisted her lime-green handbag onto her shoulder. "I gotta go find that girl and clean up some messes. Point me toward the beach."

"I want to help you find her."

Haven smiled at her. "Sweetie. I say this in the nicest possible way. You're fired. Celine doesn't want you working for her any longer—she'll pay out the contract, but she's done." She put out a hand and touched Elisa's shoulder. "Don't take it personally. There are very few of us who haven't been fired yet by Celine Carr, and the ones who haven't, wish we had."

Fired.

The word hung between them. And hung some more, while Elisa waited to be unhappy about it.

She wasn't.

She was relieved, light as air with it. She half wanted to thank Haven. This was a surprise. At some point on the beach, without realizing it, she'd let go of her need to save the weekend. Maybe it was around the time Brett had reminded her of that winter night. Their crazy-tall snowman had gotten a front-page photo in the college newspaper, and over the next few days people had come out of the dorms to see it, take pictures and climb on it. They'd even adorned it with hats and scarves.

But that night, it had been just Brett and Elisa and their giant creation. Brett had boosted her up the front of the snowman so she could poke the mittens and gloves into the snowman's face, and then he'd lowered her down the front of his body in such a way that for just a second, it had seemed like a romantic scene in a movie. A prelude to something.

Only of course, it hadn't been.

That was a long time ago, and yet the snowman had managed to become a prelude to an encounter with Brett at last. She was okay with being fired because it meant

there was no reason for her not to sleep with Brett—
which she planned to do as soon as possible.

She glanced over at Brett, and he smiled at her with
a hint of suggestion that warmed her like the sun on
white sand.

"You know what you need to do now?" Haven asked.
"You need to take that hot man of yours and go have a
really great Caribbean weekend."

Had Haven read the look that had passed between
them? It felt like she was giving Elisa permission. Elisa's heart started to beat faster. She could walk away
from this, and she could throw good sense like ashes
into the sea, and she could screw Brett's brains out.

"Thank you. And I'm sorry." She was sorry she
hadn't been able to make Rendezvous famous in a good
way, and she was even sorrier she hadn't been able to
help Celine or Haven.

Haven laughed. "Forget about it. Enjoy yourself.
Now, will you introduce me to your man?"

Elisa shook her head. "He's not my man. He's just
an old friend."

Haven tilted her head. "He isn't looking at your ass
like an old friend. Well, let me clarify that. He's looking at your ass like it's an old friend. Just not like you're
an old friend."

Elisa laughed. "He's a connoisseur."

"One of those, huh? Those are perfect for a Caribbean weekend. Do I get to meet him?"

At Elisa's gestured invitation, Brett came over and
shook Haven's hand. "Pleasure to meet you," he told her.

"Ditto."

"I'm sorry—"

"Shut up, the two of you," said Haven cheerfully.
"Quit apologizing and point me toward that beach already."

AFTER THEY DEPOSITED Haven on the beach and said goodbye, they once again climbed the long flight of stairs to the resort. Brett took Elisa's hand. His thumb moved over her palm, sending sparks of sensation through her. She tried to free herself, but he only gripped her hand more tightly.

"I'm feeling a tiny bit weird about walking away," she admitted.

"You're not walking away. Celine doesn't want your help, and Haven doesn't need your help."

She let him tug her close and nestle her under his arm. It felt parched-woman-in-desert-finds-oasis good. It did make walking up the stairs tougher, though.

"It's not your job to save Celine from trouble or disappointment," he continued, "or whatever you think is going to happen to her. It's never been your job."

"Then what? There's no point in having a dating coach? You should just go out there and bash around and hope for the best?"

"Did I say that? No. All I'm saying is that playing it safe isn't the only way to date. You don't want your clients to date jerks, which is admirable, but if you make that decision for them, you're protecting them too much. Let's face it, love isn't safe. It's a disaster. It's a tightrope walk without a net. You think you can be the net, but what you're doing is taking all the thrill out of the walk."

"And you're the expert."

A hint of color in his face told her she'd struck home. "Maybe."

"It feels wrong to walk away, like I'm leaving before the end of a movie."

"Nah," he said easily. "More like deciding you'd rather watch a play than direct it. You'll still find out what happens. You just won't be mucking around in the results. You can sit back and enjoy."

"I'd rather muck."

He laughed. "I can see that. Back in the day you had a higher tolerance for letting the world unfold, you know."

She had.

"You used to always say, 'I just can't wait to see what happens next.' Generally about things you had control over but wished you didn't."

"I used to say that?" Elisa furrowed her brow.

"Usually when it was 2:00 a.m. and you had a paper due the next morning, and you hadn't started it yet."

"Oh, I was bad about that."

"You were. You did it all the time. And then you'd come to my room to see if I wanted to play Scrabble, and when I said, 'What about the paper?' you'd say, 'Papers are what write themselves while you're busy doing other things.'"

She grinned.

He nudged her arm. "You did. And then you'd write them at like 5:00 a.m. and get better grades on them than I ever did."

Oh, God, she remembered. Liters of Mountain Dew and French-pressed coffee and junk food from the vending machine. The feeling that *what happened next* was only vaguely her responsibility, even if those were her hands on the keyboard. She would have said, "I can't wait to see what happens next," and "Papers are what write themselves while you're busy doing other things," and, probably, as dawn approached, "Carpe diem."

She shook her head in wonder. "I had more of a spirit of adventure back then."

"It takes a pretty big spirit of adventure to start your own business."

"I hope I can hang *on to* my business." She laughed darkly. "I guess—I can't wait to see what happens next."

"Thatta girl."

They crested the top step and followed a path that twisted through gardens full of blooming cacti and succulents. She'd never been a fan of the rubbery, spiny, low-lying plants, but she had to admit, they were beautiful and fragrant in bloom—flowers in every color, their beauty more obvious against the starkness of the greenery.

"The other thing you used to say all the time that I really liked was, 'Are you with me?'"

She laughed. "Oh, God, yes! 'Because if you're not with me, you're against me!'"

"That's right. I still say that sometimes. I usually try to give you credit."

"You quote me?"

"I quote you," he affirmed, the crinkles at the corners of his eyes appearing, the dimple opening in his cheek.

They arrived at his building and stepped into the lobby, where the sudden darkness temporarily blinded her, and she had to stop to get her bearings. "This way," he said, taking her arm and leading her to the elevator. He didn't bother to ask if she was coming up with him, and she didn't try to play coy.

Elisa waited until they were in the elevator to say, "I guess Celine's not still pining for you."

He mimed distress. "My heart is wounded."

"That's your ego that hurts."

"On the plus side," he said, leaning back against the elevator wall, "if she's not interested in me, I'm free to play the field." His gaze worked its way from her feet up to her face, lingering on the parts of her that were already warm and tingly. Her breath sped up, and her mouth got dry. The stolen moisture pricked to the surface between her legs.

I want to have sex with him, she thought. *I'm going to have sex with him.*

The thought made her laugh.

"What?"

Instead of answering, she let her own gaze sweep over his abs and chest and lickworthy biceps. And then she realized that what she really wanted was to stare at his mouth, so she let herself do that, too.

He came off the wall like a shot, grabbed her with no gentleness whatsoever and kissed her. His arms wrapped around her hard, he tilted his head to deepen the kiss, and his hands slid up her back and neck, yanking the elastic out of her hair. The kiss was slick, sweet and velvet, a headlong falling-in. She let her body melt against his, breasts against chest, belly against belly, her pelvis rocking against the hot, steely length of him. This. This was what she had wanted. Not just all morning, not just since she had first seen him on the plane yesterday, but forever.

He backed her against the wall of the elevator and slid a knee between hers, and she groaned and pressed her hips harder to him, trying to own him. To brand him. It was impossible, she knew, to claim him, but she would try to make it so he couldn't forget or let her go. Her hands tugged at his hair, swooped to grab his ass, took leisurely tours of the long muscles of his back, kneading. He growled into her mouth, and the sound vibrated every tender part of her.

The elevator pinged to a stop, and the doors parted. He broke the kiss, scooped her up like she weighed nothing, carried her out of the elevator and down the hall. He propped her on wobbly legs, and she clung to his arm while he unlocked and opened the door, lifted her up again, kicked the door shut with his foot and deposited her on the bed, then knelt over her. His eyes were dark and full of dirty plans. "You have no idea how much I've wanted to do this."

"I have some idea."

He began touching her with a peculiar tenderness that made her throat close up. He touched her hair and her face—her cheek, her lips, even her eyelids—and she realized she wanted to cry. He was exploring her, as if finally learning something he'd always wanted to know. Her body tingled all over, even though his touch stayed innocent. Jawline, throat, collarbone. Her breasts tightened, her nipples hardening against the lace cups of her bra.

If she already wanted to cry, how was she going to feel if she let him inside her? She might break into a thousand pieces, and she might not be able to put herself back together again. She should stop him, but she couldn't. There was an ache in her chest, between her legs, everywhere in her, an empty space that needed to be filled.

She slipped her hand into the softness of his hair and drew him down for another one of those deep, dark, consuming kisses. The emptiness in her chest seemed to grow and swell, taking over, as he laid the whole length of his hard body over hers, taking care not to crush her but still swallowing her up with the heat and solidity of his naked chest and bare legs.

"Can we get this off you before I chew it off?" He settled back on his knees, took the hem of her T-shirt and drew it up over her head. "God, Elisa," he breathed.

He took his time drinking her in while she squirmed under his gaze. Then he put out a surprisingly tentative hand and stroked his thumb along the upper edge of her bra's lace. "You have the most perfect breasts *ever*."

"I'm going to take that as a high compliment, coming from you."

He grimaced, and she was immediately sorry for spoiling the moment. "I'm not thinking about other women right now." He made it a reprimand. "You shouldn't, either."

She shook her head. "It's hard not to." *Particularly,* she added in her head, *when the woman you originally chose to spend this weekend with has architecturally marvelous breasts.*

As if he could read her thoughts, he returned his attention to the place where he was teasing above her left nipple, drawing it to attention without even making contact. "Perfect size. So round. Insanely, perfectly creamy skin. Makes me want to—"

Instead of finishing the sentence, he dipped his head and put his mouth where his thumb had just been. She felt his tongue flick out, teasing the same not-quite spot. It made her want to scream. It made her want to arch her back and thrust her breast, bra and all, into his mouth.

Just when she felt like she couldn't stand it another second, he brushed the lace away and sucked her nipple in. Sensation shot through her, centering itself between her legs. She whimpered.

"Like that?" He peeked up at her, his mouth still on her. "Want more?"

She nodded fervently. Any impulse she might have had to put an end to this was long past. She wanted him—more of what he was doing, the tongue working the nipple that he was holding between his teeth, the palm that was sliding down her belly, the fingers that were working the button of her capris and the hard length of him pressed against her thigh. He was *big*. No wonder he had such widespread appeal.

He got the button free and slid his hand into her panties, his fingers parting her curls and finding her hot and wet. She couldn't remember the last time she'd been this wet, a trickle she could feel. Her attention was split between that hungry mouth on her nipple and the intense pleasure of his fingers playing near her opening, moving up to stroke her clit, down again to swoop up her moisture and spread it, smoothing over her. She caught herself humming, and he looked up, too, and smiled at her. The old Brett smile that had made her love him to begin with.

Her craving for him had grown, filling her chest, and she realized that her hands, without her noticing, had been all over him, squeezing every muscle she could reach, stroking over expanses of smooth skin, tugging absently at the waistband of his shorts. He lifted up to let her have her way with the shorts, and—

She discovered he wore nothing underneath them. He was about to dive back into his work when she said, "Wait, I want to look at you."

He knelt and let her look her fill. A nest of brown curls, his balls drawn up tight, and his cock big and proud, a good-looking specimen—a little darker than the rest of his skin and curved slightly toward his belly. She reached out and felt the satin-over-steel texture of him. He made a sharp noise and drew back. "Not a good idea right now. Not if you want me to be any use to you. And I think you do. If this is any indication—" He dipped his fingers again. "You are so wet. So sweet. Can I tell you something?"

She nodded.

"I dream about you."

That was unexpected and caused a frisson of pain and joy through her chest. "Me?"

"You. Ever since you disappeared, and refused to return my calls and emails. Can't stop. And it's always like this." He indicated their state of nakedness, arousal, intimacy. "Only this is actually better. I'm going down," he said abruptly, and slid himself down the length of her body, taking her capris and panties with him.

He dreamed about her. Like this. That altered her whole worldview in an instant, transforming the achiness in her chest to something different—joy and longing.

She spread her legs for him. Like his kiss in the elevator, he didn't ease in. He plunged zero-to-sixty, whole mouth on her, tongue in her, lapping. She tossed her head back and forth on the pillow. If he kept that up, she was going to come in about ten more seconds, and she grabbed his shoulders to stop him. "I want to come with you inside me."

He half threw himself off the side of the bed, yanked his wallet from his shorts, and regained the bed with a victorious expression and a condom. He opened the packet and rolled on the condom, amping up the heat that had hold of her. She was half wild, wanting him in her. He positioned himself, and she grabbed his shoulders and thrust up to meet him.

"Easy."

"Tease," she said, and he laughed again.

He held back, taunting her. "What do you want?" Just the tip of him was at her opening.

"You!"

"What about me?"

"All of you. In me. Now."

He moved forward, an inch of him spreading her, opening her. The ache eased infinitesimally, then roared back. "How's that?"

Her only consolation was that he asked it through gritted teeth, and she could see that every muscle in his body was taut.

"More. All of you."

"Like this?" Another inch, and he held steady, but she could see the fierceness, the clenched jaw, lines of strain in his face.

She squeezed him, and he lost it and sank deep into her on a groan. She wrapped her arms and legs around him so he couldn't escape and rubbed herself against him as best she could.

He pulled back a little and reseated himself against her. It was perfect, the tug, the pressure, the angle. She said, "You don't even have to move. I'm going to—"

Only he apparently was no longer capable of holding himself in check, because he thrust into her and withdrew almost completely before thrusting again, his face openly needy, the cords in his neck standing out. And then she was coming like a freight train, her whole body wracked with it, and he gave a surprised yelp and tensed in release, shaking against her as he breathed her name.

Somewhat later he said, "I will make it last longer next time. I promise."

She laughed, amusement and pleasure at his use of the phrase *next time.* "It lasted long enough."

"Still. A man's got pride."

He withdrew carefully and went to the bathroom. When he came back, he settled himself beside her, one arm and one leg thrown over her, warming her. She glowed from head to toe, bright, boneless, dopey with pleasure.

Sunlight streamed into the room around the edges of the gauzy curtains, and she basked in the warmth pouring off his body, his dazed smile, the slow travel of his fingertips over her arm and shoulder.

At the same time, she was aware of a countdown that had started in her own head. She'd seen it before with him, so many times. So many women in college, so many women in New York. At first she'd rooted for him to succeed, to change his ways. This one's the one, she'd think. Later she'd place bets with herself on how quickly the sand would sift through the hourglass. A day? A week? Two?

And now she was the one on the clock, the one whose timer was slowly doling out her share. Steady, and relentless, ticking down the hours, the minutes, the seconds.

Measuring the time before Brett moved on.

12

HE WANTED MORE. He'd *never* wanted more until now. Never. That was the reason he was, as Elisa put it, a twenty-four-hour man. He worked himself into a lather wanting to have sex with a woman, but once it was over, it was over. He tried his best not to be a jerk about it. He didn't sneak out before dawn or anything like that, but the previous urgency would always be *gone*. He couldn't get it back. He could perform again, if she requested his services, but he couldn't *care*. It didn't matter, one way or another to him. All the fun, all that hot internal pressure, had fled.

If anything, the heat and longing was *worse* now. She was dozing in his arms, her breath buzzy, just shy of a snore, and he wanted more of her. He looked at the clock. Ten, maybe fifteen, minutes had elapsed since he had pulled out of her and tossed the condom, but he was already thinking about what he wanted to do to her next. Take his time, this round, going down on her. Lick all her folds and spend a good long while just lavishing affection on her clit. She was *sweet*. He'd dip his tongue into her, gathering her sweetness and giving it back to her. And when she was ready again—tipping her hips and making those little half purr, half moan noises that were his new "on" switch—he'd slide inside her and build her slowly up to another one of those screaming climaxes.

She shifted against him, her thigh pressing his erection. "Wake up," he whispered.

She opened her eyes.

"Could you do that again?" he murmured close to her ear.

"Are you kidding?" She rolled and pressed the length of her body against his. She was much softer than he had imagined. The contradiction between her leanness and strength, and her softness was part of what had undone him. "Any time."

He traced her cheekbone with his fingertip. "I want to show you that I can be more thorough."

She smiled, and the familiarity of that smile, the sense of coming back to something long lost, made his heart hurt. "Okay. That sounds good. Do I just lie back and enjoy?"

He tucked a few kisses into the crook of her neck, and she moaned.

"You don't seem like the kind of girl who is contented to lie back and enjoy. You seem like the participatory sort."

Her expression grew very serious. "Is that okay? I know you said not to think about the other women, but I've never been with anyone who's been with as many women as you have—at least not knowingly—and it's really hard to not feel like I'm being compared."

"You are being compared. And you're winning." Now he was drawing concentric circles on one breast, spiraling his way in toward her upright nipple.

She squinted one eye at him. "But you have a golden tongue, which makes it hard to believe it when you say stuff like that."

He halted his drawing project. "Believe it."

She shook her head.

"No. Really." He wanted to tell her what he'd been thinking, about how he never wanted repeats but now he did. He could have sex with her for hours. All day long. Day after day.

Not very romantic, though, when he imagined saying it out loud. And meanwhile she was looking at him and shaking her head. Laughing.

I want more. I can't get enough. I can't get enough of you.

Where was the golden tongue when he really needed it? Frozen. It worked just fine when he didn't mean it, but now it wouldn't come to his aid.

She stopped laughing and looked at him with those tawny brown eyes, her lips slightly parted. She licked them, and he felt a jolt, an outrageous surge of desire for her. He began to kiss her, much more tenderly this time than he had earlier. Nipping and nibbling, soothing with his tongue, fitting himself properly to her. The kisses fell into a rhythm, long periods of savoring, pulling back, beginning again, and then she was tasting him, plunging her tongue deep into his mouth in a way that made him crazy with need. He had her pinned, and it was all he could do to hold off from driving into her; he wanted so badly to slake his desperation. But he held himself in check and let the insanity build.

The problem was, he didn't want to let go of her mouth to fulfill his plan of sliding down her body. He couldn't let go of her mouth. It was his anchor. So she got there first. She slid herself down, her mouth burn-

ing the length of his torso until she stopped and looked
up at him, questioningly, and he said, "Oh, Jesus, yes,
please," and she took the head of his cock in her mouth,
her tongue wrapping around him, finding all the little
crevices and tender spots, and then—how was it possible that she had taken him that deeply? As she herself
liked to point out, he had been with a lot of women, and
he was pretty sure that no one's lips had ever been that
far down his cock. And she was moving up and down
on him, too, letting out little moans of what sounded
like unfeigned enjoyment. He made himself hold as still
as possible, not wanting to gag her or force himself on
her, but she showed no signs of anxiety or concern, and
he could feel the back of her throat against the tip of his
cock. If she kept it up, he was going to come.

"Get back up here," he said. Well, he tried to say it.
He couldn't find his breath, and he wasn't sure that what
came out of his mouth was actually English.

She shook her head. He could feel her tongue along
the underside of his cock, slick and strong, and driving
him closer and closer to the edge.

"I want to be inside you." The words came out stam-
mered and broken.

She let him go, but only long enough to say, "Tough
luck." And then she was down on him again, her hands
clutching convulsively at his ass, pulling him deeper,
and aside from the pure perfect sensation of it, her complete self-assurance and raw sexiness undid him. The
tension built from everywhere in his body and concen-
trated itself where her tongue stroked him, and he came
in her mouth with a long cry that was halfway between
triumph and desperation.

She swallowed every drop and then crawled back

up the length of him, dropped her head on his chest and said, "Ha!"

"Not fair," he said, when he could talk.

She shrugged, her shoulder moving against his sweaty chest. "I wanted to show you I could be more thorough." She sounded dead serious, but when she lifted her face, he could see that she was laughing. He wrapped his arms around her and dragged her back down.

I can't get enough of you.

But the words wouldn't come.

SHE STOOD LOOKING at herself in the mirror in Brett's bathroom. Her eyes sparkled, her cheeks were pink, and her mouth was red and swollen. She touched her puffy lower lip, remembering the feel of Brett's teeth on it with a shiver.

I shouldn't have done that.

Not that it hadn't felt good. Not that it hadn't satisfied some deep, pent-up need. But it had unleashed something, a bottomless pit of longing. She wanted to go back into the main room, wrap her fingers around his muscled arms and beg him to be hers.

Now that she'd made love to him, she knew it wasn't enough. All those years, when they'd been friends in college and afterward, some part of her must have known that once she got started, she'd never be able to stop. That was why she hadn't let anything happen between them. That was why she had run away, years ago, when the incident with Julie had given her a reason to.

She washed her face slowly with warm water and a washcloth, reveling in the gentle scrape of terry over her hypersensitive skin. She wanted a shower, badly, but she knew if she ran the shower, he'd want to come in with her, and she wasn't sure she could take more. More nakedness, more rawness, more need.

She wanted to leave before he could peel back her additional layers or expose her still-delicate emotions.

She came out of the bathroom to find him sleeping on his belly on the bed, his arms and legs sprawled out. She couldn't help smiling. The sight of him like that clenched at her heart. She got dressed, never taking her eyes off him, praying that he would stay asleep.

She slipped out of the room without waking him, tugging the door silently shut behind her. Before she could take her hand off the knob, another door opened several rooms down, and Morrow stepped out. He saw her and waved, an economical gesture that went with the way he talked. There was nowhere to go. She had to continue down the hall in that direction and hope he didn't put two and two together or want to make anything of it. She also had to hope that she and Brett hadn't made enough noise to carry down the hall and that Morrow hadn't come knocking at any point during their time together. Would he have stood outside the door, listening?

She was probably being paranoid. "Hi, Morrow," she said, as casually as she could, hoping she didn't look and smell like sex. She'd tied her hair back and cleaned herself up, but she felt permanently altered by what had passed between her and Brett, as if anyone looking at her could see what had happened and how she'd changed.

"Elisa." A tight nod. "Find Celine?"

That made her realize she had to tell Morrow that the weekend was officially over. "No. Well. Her publicity guru has taken over. The video's off. She's romantically interested in that guy, the paparazzo she was singing with."

Morrow's normally pleasant face formed itself into a sneer. Freelance videographer was clearly, to his mind, a higher life form than paparazzo.

"Anyway, so we're not making the video. I'll pay you for your time, whatever percentage of the total you think is fair."

He frowned at that.

Her heart kicked up. "I assume you're comfortable killing it? Name your price."

The frown eased. "Will do. Need to think a bit."

"Okay, then. That's good. Thanks, and I'm sorry about this."

He shrugged, as if to say, *Celebs—what can you do?*

She put out her hand, and he shook it. They walked together to the elevator and rode down together. She felt like an entire lifetime had elapsed since she'd ridden the elevator up a couple of hours ago.

When she got back to her room, there was no sign of Celine, and she had to remind herself that it wasn't her problem.

She took a scalding hot shower, letting the water run for a long time after she'd finished shampooing her hair and soaping her body to remove all traces of her lapse in judgment.

But of course, she couldn't make it go away, just as she couldn't stop wanting to run back to his room and throw herself into bed with him, beg him for more time, more closeness, more commitment. All she could do was wash away the physical traces of their lovemaking, get this damn weekend over with, and hope she could return to New York and put her life back together in some way that made sense.

The good news was, the way she felt about Brett had erased nearly all her emotions about the fate of Rendezvous.

The bad news was, she had no idea what was going to erase her emotions about Brett.

13

SHE HAD JUST dried off and gotten dressed when she heard a knock on the door. It was Brett.

He glared at her. "You left!"

"I needed some space."

His face softened into hurt. He was not used to being left. She wondered if he'd ever woken up to find a woman gone. She was not proud to be the first, but there was a small savage part of her that was glad she'd left before he could.

She pushed the door open wider to let him in, then pulled it shut behind him.

He was still wearing the same clothes, as if he'd simply pulled them on and come to find her. "Why?"

How was she supposed to answer that? *Because you can't give me what I want, and I need to stop wanting you to.*

How would he answer, if their situations were reversed? If she came to him, demanding to know why he'd gotten dressed and disappeared in the middle of the night? She took a stab. "This bed's more comfortable."

"You regret it?"

Of course he wouldn't let her off the hook. He didn't

pull punches. It was part of what she loved about him. She shook her head. "I just—can't."

He turned away, tension hard in the lines of his hunched up shoulders and back.

"It was good," she told the back of his neck. "It was better than good. It was amazing. But I—I'm not your type."

He turned. His eyes were bleak. "What's my type?"

"One-night stand."

This time he didn't deny it, and he didn't get angry.

She crossed the room to the balcony, and he followed. They stood, hands on the railing, looking out at the ocean. It was easier to breathe out there with the sun shining and the salty sea breeze ruffling their hair.

He spoke to the water. "Maybe that's my usual type, but not this time."

She sighed. "I don't trust it." She had almost said *I don't trust you.*

"I don't trust it, either."

She glanced up at him, surprised, and found him watching her intensely.

"So maybe it would be better if we—?" she said.

"No. You can't just run away."

This was not at all how she'd expected this to go. This reversal of the natural order. She'd spent so many years hoping he'd change, and she'd sworn she'd never do it again. And now he was pleading with her, and her heart wanted to believe it.

But she knew better. "Why shouldn't I? I watched you date for years. Woman after woman. No one lasted longer than a month."

"You gave me twenty-four hours last time," he said darkly.

"I was exaggerating." There had been a few women

he'd gone on multiple dates with, if she was being fair. But no one serious. Not ever. "I saw how you were. Why would I think I'd be any different? None of *them* were."

"That was different. A different time."

A different time. She'd wanted him to say, *You're different.*

He hadn't known how she felt about him back then. And she wasn't sure she ever wanted him to know. It was bad enough, feeling this way and doubting he could ever return her feelings. It would be humiliating if he knew she'd wanted him all those years when he'd been busy screwing half the college campus and a solid chunk of the population of Manhattan island.

"I'm changing. I know you don't think people can change, but I'm asking you to give me a chance."

"Brett?"

"Yeah?"

"What do you really want from me? Because if you just want to have sex with me again, you could probably talk me into that without feeding me a whole pile about the future."

If she were honest with herself, if she were brutally frank with him, maybe that would keep disaster at bay. Maybe that would draw the lines, erect the fences, that would protect her heart.

At a distance, the sea broke over a rock beneath its surface, a persistent splash of white in the blue. She kept her gaze on it.

"What if I want more than that?" His voice was a harsh whisper.

"Don't go there. You might think you do now, but you don't. And I'm telling you, you don't have to promise me more to get what you want. I don't want you to promise me more. I don't want there to be bullshit between us."

"It's—"

Her heart raced. He was going to deny it. He was going to say, *It's not bullshit.* He was going to say—

Instead, he put his hands on her waist and turned her, then slid his hand up to cup her breast. He made a small sound in the back of his throat that she could feel between her legs. When he kissed her, his mouth was the most tentative it had been yet, which was sexy in a way she didn't want to analyze. His thumbs moved back and forth over her nipples through the thin T-shirt and lacy bra, and she gasped.

He wrapped his arms around her. Pulled her close and molded her body to his. She felt his lips in her hair. He was warm and smelled so good she wanted to sink her teeth into him.

They stayed that way for a while, her cheek resting against his shoulder. Then it wasn't sustainable any more. Their bodies heated up. The air around them shimmered with their desire. The places where they were touching scalded and sent long spikes of sensation to all the parts of her that knew the score. She sighed. "Why is it like this?"

"I don't know. It's like a permanent high simmer. And that's with you holding perfectly still like that. God help me if you move. Or make a noise."

"Any noise?"

He shifted down against her, so the hard length of him found her inner thigh, and she made a sound that wasn't quite a sound, more a caught breath.

"That one especially."

She tilted up her face so that when he brought his mouth down, it felt like they were sliding and locking into place.

He broke the kiss. "What would you say if I said I needed a shower?"

"I just had one."

He took a handful of her damp hair. "Maybe you need another one."

"You mean maybe I'm a dirty girl?"

"That's what I mean."

"I'd say you're probably right." And she followed him into the bathroom, knowing she was probably crazy but accepting, at least for the moment, that it wasn't the kind of insanity whose grip she knew how to break.

HE RAN THE WATER while she stood and admired him, the big broad muscles across his upper back, the deep groove of his spine, the dimples in his perfect, hard ass. His legs were covered with dark brown curls of hair, and there was something secret and delicious about seeing his cock and balls from behind, something animal that made her want to grab and maul.

He stepped into the shower/tub combo. "C'mere," he said.

She followed him in and stood just outside the spray, watching as he rinsed himself under the hot water, his hair plastering itself down. His chin was tipped up so she could admire the long line of his throat, the knot of his Adam's apple, the cords in his neck. The hard male curves of his pecs covered in curly hair, the ridges of his abs. But mostly the abandon on his face, his blissful worship of the hot water. She liked watching him with his eyes closed, as if that way she could see his true self without him having access to any of hers, as if he were safe for her that way.

He held his arms open, and she went in. The water was hot, but not as hot as his body, and the roughness of his body hair, the trickle of water everywhere on her already sensitive skin, lit up the rest of her nerve endings. She wanted to lick him, so she did, first his collarbone, then his throat, then his jawline. He grabbed her face with more force than she suspected he'd intended and pressed his open mouth to hers.

She groaned, and he kissed her, hard and hot, the slick contact and the wet of the water joining the sheen between her legs to make one continuous tease. A connected sensation she couldn't escape, not even when she broke off the kiss to gasp, "Holy—"

He put the fingers of one hand in her mouth, slid the fingers of the other between her legs. As if he felt the connection, too, was drawing the line she'd felt but hadn't articulated. And the water still spilled down, and sensation was drawing up in her too fast. She was going to come against his fingers in a second, and she wanted it to last longer.

She could feel him, hard against her belly, at the juncture of her thighs, a threat and an invitation.

She pushed away his fingers in her mouth with her tongue, moved his hand from between her legs and picked up the soap. She lathered up her hands and smoothed the suds over the planes of his chest and abs, the solid feel of him a message that traveled straight from her hands to her core. She dropped her hands lower and grasped his cock, a slick, soapy up-and-down slide. Worked him hard and tight, drawing her fist over his swollen head.

"Lise," he said, and tilted to lean against the tiled wall.

She watched his head emerge again from her hand, thick and hard, slightly darker than the rest of him, and disappear again, and then she knew what she wanted.

"You do it."

"Better. When. You. Do."

"I want to watch you."

He took over, his grasp even tighter than hers had been, mean-looking, harsh, like the groans he was making now, his jaw tight, the muscles in his chest strung. There was red heat rising blotchily into his face now, and she saw a flicker of something, almost pain, move into his expression.

"Do it," she instructed. "Come."

She moved close, and he came, hot spurts against her thigh, his body rigid against her, her name broken and half-coherent on his tongue.

He'd been holding her arm too tightly with his free hand, and he let go abruptly and turned his face into the wall, panting. One hand a hard fist. The muscles of his ass clenched.

After a moment he turned back. "Jesus."

"Nice work."

"I want to mess you up like that."

"You see that showerhead?" She gestured above them. The shower nozzle was the extensible kind.

His eyes lit. "Lie down."

She lay on the shower floor, and he unhooked the nozzle and knelt between her legs.

"Temperature okay?"

She felt it with her hand and nodded. Her body was drawn tight just thinking about what he was about to do. Then he did it. He started with the spray at a distance.

"How's that?"

"Oh. Good." The spray was perfect, not too harsh, not too light. Nothing else, not even a vibrator, could send that many individual tingles through every swollen part of her. She could feel micromuscles tightening in her chest and belly. He reached for her hard nipples, but she pushed his hand away. "You'll make me come in a second if you do that."

He changed the angle a little, and she purred her approval.

"Hot," he grunted. "Do you do this at home?"

"Sometimes. I don't have the extensible kind, so it's hard to get the angle and the pressure—oh—"

He'd brought the spray a little closer, and suddenly she couldn't think. He was watching her so intently, his own pleasure in hers evident. He spread her a little more. The spray was so intense on her clit, the sensation building so fast, and it was so, so, good—

"Brett!"

He dropped the sprayer in the bottom of the shower and put his hand where it had been, two fingers deep inside her, his thumb over her clit, the pressure and surety of his hand, something to surge against, the perfect counterpoint to what he'd broken free in her body. And his mouth was on hers, too, kissing, sucking, licking, while the last of the ripples and flutters subsided.

"That was—" But she seemed to be at a loss for words.

"That looked good." He grinned.

"Oh, my God."

He laughed. "That's what we like to hear."

"Thank you."

"Thank the resort's water pressure."

"No, whatever you were doing with your hand at the end there. Was perfect. And your mouth. Made me feel like—" She hesitated. It was hard to say out loud. "—like I was coming in every cell in my body."

He was still kneeling between her legs, his cock stiffening at her words. Water from the abandoned nozzle swished against her thigh and sluiced down the drain. "I almost came all over you, watching."

"Mmm." The visual of that made her sex clench, despite how thoroughly she'd dispelled her tension.

"Mind if I get a condom?"

"Please."

He stepped out of the shower and retrieved one from the bathroom vanity. In the meantime she stood and replaced the shower nozzle, rinsing herself off. Her body was still throbbing, hot and swollen. She slid her hand down, and felt the heat and moisture. "You're going to like this," she called to him.

"Wasn't worried I wouldn't." He stepped back into the shower, condom in place, a prodigious display of size that made her mouth and her core feel empty and achy. "Turn around. Put your hands up on the wall."

With other men, this position had always seemed incredibly impersonal to her, but with Brett, now, it was different. He pressed his chest against her back and settled his face beside hers.

"Put your foot up here," he said, gesturing to the edge of the tub, and she obeyed. She felt his erection against her back, and the breath went out of her as heat—anticipation—knifed through her belly. Having Brett *almost* penetrate her was as good as having sex with most men. She could probably make herself come again in a few seconds, just from the promise of that cock against her.

But he didn't deliver right away. He put his hand on her belly. "You're so beautiful," he murmured.

Desire expanded in her, like a stop-action movie of a flower opening, and she whimpered as he slid his hand up, up, until his teased the sensitive underside of her breast. He lifted and molded it, his fingers sometimes tripping over her nipple as if by accident, and she wanted him to stop and pay attention there, but he wouldn't. She pushed her breast into his palm, and he laughed, low and amused.

"Want something?"

The tip of his cock slid through the wetness he'd called out of her. Then he was in her, a hard, hot pressure on some perfect spot, and his hands were on her breasts, his thumbs and forefingers rolling her nipples, and she was making a low, dark sound she'd never heard herself make before.

"You like that?"

He moved against her, slowly, easily, wooing that supersensitive spot, teasing it. The tile was cold under her hands, the water was pouring over her head, and she closed her eyes and lost herself completely to the sensation. He jacked the water temperature. She hadn't realized it had gotten cooler, but now steam rose. His cock was filling her, stretching her, touching that crazy-good spot he'd found, because of course she'd have to have some magic button that only Brett knew about. There was that little justice in the world.

He slid one hand over her hip, the other still tormenting her breast, and found her clit. The touch was so faint it was more a tease than a sensation, just a brush and tingle, until it was way more, a mad rush of heat and wetness and building tension, connecting all the most sensitive spots on her body, and then, as he wrapped his arms tight around her and braced them away from the wall with his elbows, she was coming again, and so was he, and the sound of him calling her name got lost in the sound of her calling his.

14

THAT NIGHT THEY had dinner in the resort's main restaurant, seated across from each other at a small table with a cream-colored tablecloth and two flickering candles.

"Ohmigod, this is good." She slid another bite of steak au poivre off her fork and into her mouth.

He was staring at her.

"What?"

"I'm trying very hard not to find that sexy, but it's not working."

She took another bite.

"I think it's the way you drag your mouth over the fork. Or possibly the little noises you're making. They're reminding me of something else. Did you know it's practically impossible for me to be simultaneously this horny and actually hungry?"

"Are you saying my enjoyment of my meal is ruining yours?"

"I'm saying there is a serious conflict of interest within my body. At the snake brain level. *Food. Sex. No, food! No, sex!*"

"I hadn't realized there was a level of your brain above the snake brain."

"Ha. Very funny."

She realized she'd hurt his feelings. "Hey." She put her hand on his. "You know I don't mean that."

He shrugged, and she was reminded of what she'd said to him the night before, that his opinion of himself wasn't very high. She tried to think whether that had always been true. She knew he worshipped his older brothers and that he didn't see himself as being in their league. One brother made policy in the presidential administration— she'd seen his name bandied about in the press when the health-care debate had heated up—and the other managed a women's NBA team. Pretty hard-hitting, but so was a news anchor. If he was comparing himself and finding himself lacking, it wasn't on the grounds of accomplishments. It was something deeper.

Zachary, Peter and Brett had been the "smart," "athletic" and "handsome" brothers, respectively. That was before parents knew they weren't supposed to label their kids, that kids internalized those labels for life. And of course Brett wasn't the kind of guy to dwell on stuff— no way he'd blame his parents or gripe about them in therapy—but at the same time, if you'd been the "handsome" one all your life, you might keep finding evidence in the world that that was who you were—and all you were. Women who fell all over you, for example. If you believed in your heart that those women were only interested in you for what you looked like, it would be hard to convince yourself that there was more to it.

He was still watching her eat, though he was also eating his own dinner now, a pork chop slathered with apple compote.

"I know you were kidding when you said this on the plane, but I didn't become a dating coach because of you."

"I know."

"If anything, I did it because of Julie."

Her sister's name hung in the air between them.

"Because she has made such a disastrous mess out of her dating life. The same mistakes over and over again, sleeping with the wrong guy, getting her heart broken. I think stuff like that is much more obvious from the outside, and the right advice can really change everything for a woman who's in one of those bad patterns."

"That's a good reason." He took a deep breath. "Lise?"

"Yeah?"

"I didn't have sex with Julie."

"Don't." She turned away.

"What?"

"I don't want to hear it. I told Julie, when it happened, I didn't want to know anything about it. And I still don't."

"But—"

"It really doesn't matter whether you had sex with her or not. The fact remains that you took *my sister* out on a date two weeks after you kissed me. That was a really shitty thing to do."

She'd said it, acknowledged the Kiss That Would Not Be Named, and the world hadn't ended. Her heart was still beating, if faster than usual. He was still sitting across from her, possibly watching her more carefully now, as if he expected her to implode or—and this felt infinitely more likely—burst into tears.

"It was a really shitty thing to do," Brett said. "And I'm sorry. I'm really, really sorry."

"Why did you kiss me?"

It wasn't the question she'd meant to ask. She'd meant to ask, *Why did you go out with Julie?*

But it was the question that had come out of her mouth, so she guessed it was the question she most needed the answer to.

He reached across the table and took both her hands. His hands were warm and strong, and hers disappeared into the cave they formed. His eyes were dark and full of a significance she wanted to believe. She only had to let herself, and she could be completely swept away by him. They still had all of tomorrow left and tomorrow night and then—this was the part she couldn't let herself think about. What would happen when they got back to New York? Leaving St. Barts could be an ending point. And yet it was hard to imagine that she'd be ready for it to be over. Nothing about their passion for each other seemed to be leading toward a natural conclusion. It certainly hadn't felt that way in the shower this afternoon, or when they'd dried off and fallen asleep on the bed, and she'd woken to find him watching her sleep as he very slowly, very lightly, circled her hip with one finger.

"I kissed you because—because you were you. Because you were beautiful and sexy. Because I'd been not kissing you for too long. Because I couldn't not kiss you any longer."

She felt the pressure of held-back tears behind her eyes. She didn't trust herself to speak, so she just turned her hand in the cradle of his and squeezed his fingers.

She'd given enough fearful women advice that she knew what she needed to tell herself. *Take it one night at a time. One date at a time, one encounter at a time. Just because you've had your heart broken before doesn't mean it will be broken again this time.*

He smiled at her, and she smiled back. "That's a good reason."

As hard as it is, you have to have a little faith.

She'd never realized how hard that advice was to take.

THEY WALKED ON the beach after dark. Brett carried a rolled towel that he'd taken from the room, tucked under his arm, and a bottle of wine. Elisa had two stemmed glasses she'd borrowed from the bar, which was being tended now by a squat woman with corn rows. She hoped the bartender from last night was catching up on sleep.

They walked until they found a secluded cove, and then Brett spread the towel, and they sat and poured wine. It was dark, but they could see lights strung all along the shore and on boats out at sea. There was almost no breeze, only the purr of the ocean and the warmth still radiating from the sand beneath them. The smell of salt and cooling vegetation scented the air.

"To—" Brett raised a glass.

"Celine Carr," she offered.

He laughed. "To Celine. And Haven, because without Haven, we might still be chasing Celine all over the island."

They toasted and drank.

"Have you heard from them?"

"Haven caught up with the happy couple and tried to talk Celine into leaving, alone. No success. So Haven's going to stick around and keep an eye on them. Manage the media situation, keep Celine out of trouble. Apparently they went snorkeling this afternoon."

"All three of them?"

"Celine and Steve. Haven reported that she doesn't get her hair wet. She cheered them on from shore."

Brett laughed. "I'd believe that." He extended the arm that wasn't holding his glass and tugged her closer, burying his face in her hair. "You smell so good."

"It's that expensive resort shampoo."

He laughed. "Which you used three times today, right?"

"The last time I showered I just rinsed off. I started to get worried my hair would roll over and die from all the washing."

"So you're sparkly clean."

For a moment she remembered the sensation of repressing the provocative thoughts that crossed her mind, the ache in her tongue from holding back what she wanted to say to him. "No, filthy dirty," she said. The feeling of freedom that came with letting go was heady. Lowering her voice to a purr, so she could feel it everywhere, she said, "I'm wearing a skirt."

A slight hesitation and then he said, "Yeah?"

"It's dark out."

The tension she strung between them made her wet, a liquid heat that sang his name.

His voice got lower, too. "It is."

Her heart started pounding harder. Their little cove was secluded, but they could hear people walk by occasionally on the beach, and the chance of discovery was low but real. She'd never done anything like this before. "I have condoms."

Just his breathing beside her and the surf beyond. She sifted sand through her fingers and waited.

"Here?"

"Yeah."

There was a long silence.

"No pressure," she said. "We could go back to the room. If you don't want to do it here."

"Are you kidding me? Of course I want to." He grabbed her hand and clamped it down on his erection. "That's how much I want to."

Like iron under his khakis, so hard she could feel the distinct flare of the head and the ridge down his length. Her body unfurled with heat and light at the sensation.

She unbuttoned his slacks, eased them over his hips to his thighs, then freed him from his boxer briefs. He sprang up against her hand. She loved the contrast of the soft feel of his skin and the unyielding hardness underneath.

She gave him one of the condoms, stood and dropped her panties onto the towel. Then she knelt over him, facing away, her skirt spread out over them. Anyone who came close would guess immediately what was going on, but if they held still and stayed quiet, they could go undetected.

He made a strangled noise when her wetness slid against his length.

"I can't see what I'm doing, so you've got to maneuver." She lowered herself slowly.

He grabbed her hips and raised her again, then fumbled between them and tugged her back down.

"You're so wet." He proved it by filling her with a single, swift stroke, and now it was her turn to make a noise that she had to swallow.

"Holy—" he whispered. Thrusting up to meet her. "This position—"

"Don't hold back." The words crackled in the air, sounding impossibly loud even though she'd whispered them.

"I'm not. I couldn't." He was bucking against her, hitting that spot again, the magic spot that he had conjured for her earlier. The breeze had come up. It lifted strands of her hair and brushed over her heated cheeks. His hands were on her waist, raising and lowering her, his hips beneath hers lifting emphatically to drive himself home as he yanked her down. When she began to take over the rhythm, he loosened his grip and slid his hands up the front of her shirt to toy with her nipples between his fingers.

"Nngh."

"Shh."

"Unh."

"Lise, shh."

"I can't. That feels too good."

They heard voices on the beach and froze. Beneath her, his hips moved slightly, restlessly, then again, his cock throbbing. The voices came closer. He'd wrapped an arm around her and was holding her still, his lips on her ear. She realized all the shifts and twitches and throbbing were involuntary. It was too hard for him to hold still.

Oh, that was *way* too much fun.

They couldn't see the people from behind the rock that hid their revelries, but they could hear them clearly, a group of girls, laughing and talking.

She tightened her inner muscles for all she was worth, and she felt his whole body jerk against hers.

"Not. Fair." A harsh whisper against her ear.

Again, she bore down on him with all her strength. Her own muscles gave a second involuntary clench, then rippled with echoed pleasure. If she wasn't careful, she was going to be the victim of her own game.

She reached under her skirt and slicked her fingers over his balls. Behind her he made an audible noise, a grunt that was almost a groan.

"Shh," she said, with great satisfaction.

The voices had passed on. It was quiet on their stretch of the beach, but behind her, under her, he wasn't quiet, and he wasn't still. The smell of sex mingled with the scent of sea salt, and the sand was gritty under her right foot. He was pushing up as hard as he could, and she was pressing down on him, suddenly finding a rhythm that let her move against her wrist as she stroked him.

And then she shoved her other fist in her mouth, yelled silently as she came in deep, seizing waves. All the sensations, the sand, the sea, the breeze, the heat, the wet, coalesced into one thunderous moment that took her completely outside herself, and dragged a cry and long spasms from him.

"Do you think anyone heard?" she whispered, a few minutes later.

"Do you think there's anyone who *didn't* hear?"

She climbed off and turned around, and threw her arms around him. "God, Brett. I missed you." Which was kind of a funny thing to say right at that moment, because what they'd been doing hadn't been anything she could have missed. And yet it felt all of one piece—her affection for him, his joking and humor, his quickness— the sex was part of who he was, who she was, who they were together, and the fact that it had been missing from their friendship all those years seemed to make no sense now. Maybe the sex had always been there, all along, waiting for them.

"I missed you, too."

She clung hard to him, harder because she didn't know how long it would last, how long it could last, and she wanted to wring every last drop of pleasure out of it.

15

IN THE MORNING they made love again, and then they went snorkeling, swimming among the brightly colored fish and eels, and touching the leathery-smooth shell of a sea turtle. Later in the day Brett rented paddleboards for them, and they spent most of the afternoon capsizing and righting them again. After a while they realized it was more fun to tip each other over than to stay on top of the boards, and the whole thing degenerated into one big splash fight, until they were laughing and kissing. She almost cried with joy.

He took her back to his room, stripped off her bathing suit and led her to the shower, where he washed her from head to toe with gentle hands and kissed water droplets from her face until she wasn't completely sure some of them *weren't* tears.

"Lise."

Was it the beginning of a question or a plea all in itself? He was hard again—she could feel him against her belly as he washed the last of the shampoo out of her hair.

"Uh-huh?" She was having trouble drawing a full breath; she wanted him inside her so badly.

"What happens when we leave?"

She didn't ask what he meant. She'd been wondering the same thing all day. The million-dollar question.

Her body had its own opinions, and it wanted more. But she couldn't let that part of her be in charge. She had to be rational. Easier to walk away now, before she got any more invested. Everyone knew that what you did when you were on vacation didn't belong in your life back home. She was about to tell him, *What happens in St. Barts stays in St. Barts,* when he said, "I'm not ready to give you up."

His voice was low and rough. Shaky. It did something to her, softening her insides, shaking her up. She knew he could sling it with the best of them, and she didn't believe his words, but she did believe the way he said them.

She pressed her cheek against his.

Me neither, she thought.

He led her out of the shower, dried her off, laid her down on the bed and made love to her again, so slowly she melted, her whole body liquid heat, like running gold under his hands. Because he moved so slowly, and because there was no tension left anywhere in her, she built up toward climax gradually, without frustration or need to chase it. It was there, it would be there for her when she was ready for it.

He was whispering something now.

"What?"

Whatever it was, he was saying it over and over again, his body pressed close to hers, his mouth beside her ear, and she leaned back a little to get closer, to hear better. Her heart almost cracked in two when she heard what it was, his litany, his chant—

He whispered it again, right against her ear, his

breath warm as he pressed higher up into her and slowly, so slowly, pushed her off the cliff she'd been climbing into an orgasm that was like a starburst of pleasure.

"I never want to stop."

AFTERWARD, SHE CALLED a taxi and went down to the lobby. She and Brett had decided to venture into Gustavia for dinner. She stood just inside the sliding doors, waiting for him to show up, and thought about how often she'd waited for Brett.

She was sore from having sex so many times, but all she could hear was the whisper of his voice. *I never want to stop.*

Though she knew he only meant he could go all night like this, it hadn't mattered to her heart, which had heard it as a promise. His words had gotten under her skin so far that she didn't think she could ever get them out again.

I never want to stop had been good, but so had *I'm not ready to give you up.* Those were the words he'd said to her in the shower.

Even now, the echo made her melty. She'd had so much resolve before he'd said them, had almost had enough resolve to walk away from him, but he'd used the golden tongue on her, and now she had nothing.

"Oh, Elisa," she said out loud. "You need to stop being a dork."

She could see her reflection in the mirror across the lobby. She'd blown her hair dry, and for once it had cooperated with her efforts—all smooth, glossy redbrown. She wore white capris and a tight black tank top. She'd put on mascara and lip gloss.

She'd dressed up for him.

"An irredeemable dork," she said sadly.

An older couple sitting on a high-backed wooden bench looked at her funny.

She pulled out her phone and pulled up Razzle. She wanted to know how they were faring.

There were three new photos. Celine, sitting on Steve's lap, beaming into his face. His arms were around her.

She smiled, against her better judgment. They were a cute couple. Steve's dark features made a nice contrast against Celine's blond hair and pale eyes.

Celine and Steve—oh, my, God, were they paddle-boarding? They totally were. She wondered if she and Brett had just missed them. What about her ankle? That had healed up pretty damn fast. Elisa had to suspect Celine had created some extra drama on Friday night, maybe for Steve's benefit. Celine looked pretty good on her board. Steve, however, was dragging himself up out of the water, a shit-eating grin on his face, hair drenched and clinging to his forehead.

The last shot was a close-up of Celine and Steve sitting side by side on the beach, Steve's lips brushing Celine's ear. Her own skin tingled in sympathy. It looked like he was whispering something to her.

"They look like they're doing okay."

Brett had appeared at her shoulder. He grinned at her, crinkles forming at the base of his nose and at the corners of his eyes. He looked mischievous in a way that made her want to suggest that they bail on the internet café and head back to his room.

"What do you think he's saying to her?"

"Do you really want to know? I can guess." He leaned in, and she caught a whiff of mint. She wanted to lick his mouth. He lowered his voice until it was little more than a vibration against her ear. "I can't stop thinking about your mouth, and I want it all over my body. Also—holy hell, your hair smells good."

Her face heated first, then the rest of her, a surge of sensation in her belly and lower.

"I want to bury my face in it."

"Stop," she whispered. "We're going to dinner."

He just laughed.

"I called a taxi. Should be here soon."

As if on cue, a squat blue van pulled up, and she darted ahead of him to climb in back. Not looking at him made it a tiny bit easier to deny how badly she was falling for him. It reminded her of how little kids covered their eyes and thought they couldn't be seen. She snuck a look back at him. "Are you with me?" she demanded. "Because if you're not with me, you're against me."

"Oh, I'm with you, all right."

She tried not to hear any significance in those words.

The ride to town was slightly—but only slightly— less hair-raising than landing on the island had been. They were flung back and forth, until Brett put his arm around her and held her. It got harder after that not to look at him, and finally she gave in. He was gazing down at her with something that was an awful lot like what she knew was in her own expression. He couldn't fake that, could he?

But he'd been an awfully talented seducer two years ago, and he'd only had time to get better. So she turned away before he could kiss her and stared out the window. *I'm not listening, I'm not listening.*

She meant, of course, *Stupid heart, I'm not listening to you.*

In town, two-story buildings lined the narrow streets. Gustavia looked like a European city. French, or Dutch, maybe, with white-painted balconies and arched doors flung open on the lower levels.

"See those boats?" Elisa pointed to the harbor.

He laughed. "Those aren't boats. Those are yachts. Look. That one has a helicopter pad. Do you think Celine will have something like that someday?"

"If she doesn't blow it and get her contract canceled," Elisa said, feeling sorry for her hotheaded former client.

Their little café was nestled between an expensive-looking jewelry boutique and a big Gucci store. The driver let them out in front of the café, a sunlight-dappled room with a terra-cotta tiled floor and walls painted in warm shades. Brett got them a corner table with two chairs at right angles.

Hunger—the food kind—had come over her like a ton of bricks as they'd walked into the café, which smelled like garlic and wild mushrooms and expensively prepared meat. "I want arugula soup," she said from behind her menu.

"I think I need big food. No soup for me. I'm leaning toward the hangar steak."

"Why so hungry?" she teased.

He gave her a searing look in reply. Heavy lids over eyes gone from pale green to something smokier. There was nothing about him not perfectly calculated to destroy her.

He pulled his chair as close to hers as he could. "Hey."

"Yeah?" Her heart pounded, but she ignored it.

"I want you to promise me you'll let me take you to dinner when we go home. Try to make this work in New York."

She wanted that so much. But what stopped her was the familiarity of the wanting. She'd once wanted something this much, more than she wanted Celine to find the guy of her dreams, or for Rendezvous to succeed.

She'd wanted Brett Jordan to love her. She *wanted* Brett Jordan to love her.

Because she loved him.

"I am such a glutton for punishment," she said. Out loud, because he might as well know.

"Look. I know you don't think I'm capable of a relationship."

She shook her head.

"What? No, you don't think that? Or no, I'm not?"

"It's not you."

"It's not you, it's me?" he hazarded.

"No, I'm not breaking up with you. I'm just trying to explain. Why I can't do this."

"So you are breaking up with me."

"No."

"You can't do this, but you're not breaking up with me?"

"I said 'can't,' not 'won't.'"

"You'll forgive me if that distinction isn't making me feel any better."

She laughed, then wanted to cry, because he could make her laugh even at a moment like this one.

"I know it pissed you off that I hooked up with your sister."

Her eyes widened. "Is that what you think this is about?"

He was looking at her intensely. Really looking, like he was trying to find answers in her face. "You stopped talking to me right after that. What was I supposed to think?"

How was she going to say this out loud? It felt way harder than taking off her clothes for him had. If she'd been naked then, she'd be flayed after she told him the truth.

Back in the day, in the earlier years of their friendship, they had sometimes laughed together about the women who fell for him. Made fun of them. On a small college campus, word got around, and everyone knew that Brett Jordan wasn't relationship material. So what would possess women to think that would change? What would possess them to show up at his dorm room, days after a one-nighter, in skimpy lingerie under a winter coat, bound and determined to seduce him?

Elisa had argued that it was a self-respect issue. They'd rather beg to be a member of a club that didn't want to admit them than be with someone who thought they were worth it.

He was staring at her, waiting for her to explain. What could she say? Years ago, when she'd fallen for him, she'd allowed herself to be as dumb as those other women who'd put themselves through the Brett Jordan machine.

And now she'd gone and done it again.

She remembered, with icy clarity, the speech he'd given Celine in the cab Friday afternoon. The "You're better off without me" speech. Not today, but sometime soon, he'd give her that speech, too. Probably she'd get her heart broken. But that didn't mean she had to have her pride destroyed along with it. Better to stick with the story he already believed.

"Yeah. Yeah, okay. I was hacked off you went out with my sister. But no biggie. I'm over it now."

Profound relief spread over his face. "So you'll see me in New York?"

"Sure." Maybe she would. All she knew right now was that she couldn't tell him how long she'd waited for him to ask her that question. Even now, when it should have been too late, her heart beat wildly at hearing it.

Her phone buzzed in her pocket. She pulled it out. Haven.

"Hang on," she said, and exited the restaurant to take the call. The narrow avenue was lively with tourists speaking in many languages, loaded up with shopping bags, laughing and flirting. Ah, the Caribbean. Would it really be possible to maintain the magic once she and Brett returned to the real world? And he had his pick of one-night stands on a regular basis?

"Hey, Haven."

"Elisa. I need your help. ASAP. Do you have a Twitter account?"

"I don't. I keep meaning—"

"You need to be on Twitter for your business *now,* Elisa, but that's not the point. The point is that someone is live tweeting about Celine. Really creepy, intimate stuff. Convincingly intimate. Stuff you could only know if, say, you'd spent the whole weekend with her."

Elisa's heart pounded. "You think it's Steve."

"It *has* to be him."

"Oh, hell." What a mess.

"I've lost her again," Haven said. "It's been cat and mouse on and off since I've gotten here. I've texted her. I've called her. I've chased her around the resort. I've chased her around the island. I can't get through to her. Can you talk to her? Tell her it's time for this to end. She needs to go home."

"What makes you think she'll listen to me? You guys *fired* me."

"She told me to fire you in a fit of pique. She does that to everyone. But you got her to pay attention in a way I've never seen her do with anyone else. Please, Elisa, will you at least try? Call her. Text her. Get her to meet with you. Tell her what Steve's been doing. Tell her it's time to go home. I'm begging you, and I don't beg anyone."

"Of course," Elisa said. "Of course I will."

"And let me know after you've talked to her."

"You got it."

Elisa went back inside and explained to Brett what had happened.

"Steve?"

She nodded. "That bastard." Disappointment clotted her chest, and her words were unsteady. "Why did he bother to pretend? It just makes him more of a sadist."

She wasn't as angry as she would have thought she'd be, though. She recognized what she felt as a variation on grief.

She'd lost something, some briefly held hope, a little flare of optimism. She'd let herself hope that Brett had been right about Steve. He'd almost had her convinced that people deserved the benefit of the doubt. That they were capable of change.

Almost.

16

IN THE END, Elisa sent Celine a text that said, "I have something important to tell you. Where are you?" and Celine sent back a text that said, "I'm changing in my room." It was as easy as that.

She knocked on the door, and Celine admitted her, no resistance, no anger. Her hair was up in a tightly knotted towel.

Elisa didn't try to sugarcoat it or mince words. She just related exactly what Haven had said to her. Then she pulled up the brand-new Twitter app she'd loaded on her phone, and showed Celine the list of the tweets sent by @Tomorrowsnews.

Celine turned away from the sight. "We don't know that it was Steve."

"'She's a fireball in bed. Whimpers when I kiss her, begs me for it, yells when she orgasms.'"

Celine's blue eyes contained so much kicked-puppy-dog hurt that Elisa had to look away.

"I don't understand. He told me he really likes me. He told me—"

Elisa didn't want to know. She ached enough for Celine without knowing what, exactly, Steve had promised her. "He meant it at the time."

Because they always did, didn't they? Surely Brett had meant it when he had said that he couldn't get enough. That he didn't want to stop. And he had meant it when he had said he wanted to have dinner with her in New York.

It was just that, at any moment, he could stop meaning it. She'd seen him do it before.

It had hurt so much when he'd gone out with Julie, whether they'd had sex or not. She could lie to herself six thousand different ways, but it had hurt like nothing else had hurt. Because up until that moment she had told herself he was protecting their friendship by not pursuing her. She had told herself that he was attracted to her but not willing to risk what they had. Then, when he'd pursued Julie, she'd seen that wasn't true. He wasn't afraid for the friendship. He just didn't feel *that* way about her. He would never be the guy who leaped hurdles for her. He'd never say *I can't get enough,* and mean it, and mean it forever.

"I'm so, so sorry," she said to Celine. All her frustration with Celine, with the weekend, had melted away. They were two women in the same boat. Maybe Elisa had thought she was the captain once upon a time, but she knew the truth. She was bailing madly like everyone else.

Celine gazed back at her, her eyes lost and a little wild. Elisa wasn't sure what was going to happen next. Another accusation, more anger.

Celine's face crumpled.

Elisa didn't think. She just reacted, taking the smaller woman in her arms. Celine was soft and smelled like strawberries, and as soon as Elisa put her arms around her, she began to cry. And Elisa held her. It was sort of like holding her younger, more naive self, the part of her that was going to get hurt again, because there was nothing she could do to stop herself from loving Brett.

She held Celine and rocked her and whispered comfort until the tears stopped.

"I really liked him," Celine said, when she could talk again. "More than I've ever liked anyone. Do you know what one of the first things he ever said to me was? I was telling him about how Haven was rehabbing my image, and he said, 'What's wrong with your image?' And I said, 'It's slutty, I guess,' and he just looked at me, really *looked* at me, and said, 'It's human.' But I guess that was all an act. That's what he does, right? Gets celebrities to talk to him about their real selves. Makes people feel at ease."

"Yeah. I think so."

"He used me."

Elisa could only nod. She didn't want to say *I told you so* or make Celine acknowledge that she'd been warned. She stroked Celine's hair and whispered, "It's going to be okay."

"I *slept* with him. God, I have the worst judgment. The *worst*."

"No, hon. Don't beat yourself up." She was going to kill Steve if she ever got her hands on him. Wring his neck and then stomp on the limp body.

"So what do you think? Is everything I told him going to be all over the weeklies?"

"Not necessarily."

"It is. It totally freaking is."

Elisa released Celine, and the star shook her blond head like a cat trying to regain equilibrium after a humiliating fall.

"I'm going to call Haven. Will you stay?"

Elisa nodded.

Celine swiped tears and eye makeup prettily off her face. "She's gonna kill me."

"No, she won't. You didn't do anything wrong." *Except trust him,* a voice whispered in Elisa's head.

"You were right," Celine whispered. "You were totally, totally right."

"I wish I weren't." *About you, about me, about any of it.* She was surprised when her own eyes filled with tears.

Celine scrutinized Elisa for a moment. Then the star hugged Elisa again, an all-in, arms-tight, serious hug.

Neither woman said a word, but Elisa understood that this time, Celine was comforting her.

WHEN THE KNOCK came on the door, Brett opened it, searching Elisa's face for a clue about how things had gone. She mostly looked exhausted—and beautiful. Her skin had a porcelain quality, her lips were soft and pink, her eyes warm even now that her lids drooped slightly with fatigue. And then there was the long line of her throat and the expanse of clear, smooth skin above the scoop of her tank. His body made note of all of it, cued now for instant response. "How did she take it?"

She gave him the faintest quirk of those lickable lips, barely a smile. "About as well as could be expected."

"And she's ready to go home?"

"Yeah."

It was time—for Celine, and for Elisa and Brett. This would be their last night, the end of their strange, awkward, perfect weekend. And, he prayed, the beginning of something new. Something bigger. He'd never wanted anything like this before, a relationship that continued into the future, far past his own horizon.

"How are *you*?" He pushed the door shut behind her and opened his arms. "Come here."

At first, she was stiff in his arms, but then he felt her slowly letting go, softening against him. His girl. His friend. As if something in her knew where she belonged. Right here. Even if she was still as nervous about him in some ways as she'd been at the beginning of the weekend. She had agreed to date him in New York, but he could tell she didn't like it. Did it make her feel twitchy and claustrophobic, like she was the one with commitment issues?

That was okay. He would show her that she could trust him.

She came alive in his arms. She was like a new flicker of flame, her breath coming faster, her limbs moving impatiently as she tried to line her body up with his, find their best fit. And their best fit was crazily good, a near-perfect alignment, her breasts against his ribs, her hip against his rapidly hardening cock, the cradle of her thighs, soft, but with the shock of hard bone to grind against, just the hint of it driving him mad. And then there was her hair, the whole fragrant mass of it within his reach if he just dipped his head. Which he did, drawing in the deepest breath of her shampoo-and-Elisa scent he could.

Her arms twined themselves around his neck, and she lifted her mouth to his, which instantly changed the whole tenor of the interaction. It caught fire, and she moaned into his mouth, which made him lose his grasp on reality, scoop her up, and ease her back against the closed door. Her legs wrapped around his waist, and she fitted herself so the hardness of her pubic bone put maximum pressure right where he wanted it. Unfortunately she was wearing pants, and so was he, but there was no way in hell he was putting her down. Having her up like this, wedged between him and the wall, was filling him with a frantic possessiveness.

Even if she didn't know it or trust him yet, she was his, and he kept one hand behind her, supporting her, as he slid the other up the front of her shirt, tracing the curve of her breast, the insistent tightness of her nipple. He rubbed himself as gently as he could over the seam of her pants, feeling the heat through all the layers of their clothing, hearing her gasp, her rapid breathing, and she worked herself harder against his hand, her head falling against the wall. "Don't stop," she moaned.

"No," he agreed.

"It's the perfect amount of friction. It's the perfect amount of pressure."

He was torn. He wanted to give her that, and he wanted to give her more. He could make it perfect inside her, too, could fill her and still give her his body to strain against, and the thought of making perfect more perfect was too much to resist. He set her on her feet, and pushed her pants and panties down. She groped for his belt and button and zipper, yanking him open. The cool air was a relief until she started trying to climb his body, to get purchase on him, and he could feel her wetness slicking his thigh. That was too much for him to resist.

He found the condom he'd stashed in his pocket and, with her help, managed to cover himself. Then he lifted her and sank into her in almost the same motion, driving her back against the wall, wet heat replacing cool air and threatening to wrench an orgasm out of him before he was ready to give in. He closed his eyes and forced himself to think about how much it was going to cost him to renovate the bathroom in his condo, and that helped enough so that he could thrust the rest of the way into her, seating himself so deeply in her that she whimpered and began trying to wriggle against him. "Come," he commanded. "I want you to come so hard you forget your name."

She rocked and thrust, and he watched the flush climb into her face. He slid his fingers up her shirt again, wrapped his hand around the curve of her breast, took her nipple gently between his thumb and forefinger. He meant to tease only, and was shocked as hell when instead she jerked against him and cried out her release. So shocked, in fact, that he followed her, matching her long-clenching spasms with his own deep, almost painful thrusts and spurts. He leaned his forehead against the wall right next to where her head tipped back, and he listened to the duet of their breathing. His legs trembled and his arms ached, but there was no way he was letting her go. Not now. Not, if he had his way, ever.

17

SHE SLOWLY RETURNED to earth. He kept her there, against the wall, until their bodies started to cool. Then he set her down and went to toss the condom, and she hobbled, weak-kneed, to the bed and crawled under the covers.

He'd divested himself of his pants, and now he peeled off his shirt and climbed in with her, wrapping himself around her, tugging her close so his body heat soaked into her. She relaxed, unwinding, degree by degree, all the muscles she hadn't realized were stiff, all the parts of herself she'd been holding in check. All the emotions she'd kept from him. From herself.

I love you.

She'd started thinking it when he'd picked her up and pressed her to the wall. Something about the primitive, possessive way he'd held her. The way he'd *taken* her. She didn't think she'd ever been *taken* before, a command wrapped in a sacrament. *Yes, yes, yes.* And *I love you.*

Of course, she wouldn't say it. She might never say it. She could only say it if he said it first, and he would probably never say it first, because unless she was very much mistaken, it was not something he was capable of feeling. Or at least not something he was capable of admitting he felt. There had been hundreds of women before her, and she'd bet her right arm that not one of them had heard those three little words spoken aloud.

A girl could blame whatever she wanted. Maybe it was the way his parents had labeled and reduced him, never noticing him for any accomplishment other than his sunny good looks. They'd turned him into the "cute" one—and only that.

Or it could be that she'd hit the nail on the head Friday night when she'd razzed him about not thinking very highly of himself. She'd been half-kidding, but there was plenty of truth in her words. He was always jocularly knocking himself down. And maybe, just maybe, he was afraid that, if he let a woman get close to him, if he opened more than a twenty-four-hour window and let someone into the inner sanctum, she'd see what he saw: not enough.

She didn't know. And even if she was right, she didn't think she'd ever get him to admit it. He wasn't the kind of guy who went in for that sort of introspection. But whatever it was, the end result had been the man who lay spooning her, a man whose generous nature and thorough-going awesomeness had somehow never led him to love or be loved.

It made her sad for both of them.

She wished he hadn't asked to date her when they got home. She wished he hadn't given her that flimsy, stupid reason to hope. It only made things harder, would only make it hurt worse when he was done with her, when he, inevitably, moved on. And yet, as much as it would hurt later, she wanted this. Everything he could give her, as many times as he would move in her like that, fierce but also tender.

He stroked her hair, a slightly rough, definitely male hand, moving ever-so-sweetly through the strands, stopping at the slightest snare or tangle. His mouth was near her ear, and he whispered something she couldn't make out at first. Her name. Over and over. Her heart swelled with—she might as well name it—with love.

This was a buoyant, warm, dangerous feeling, so big she wanted to split open. Wanted him to split her open. That was the point—she grasped now, for the first time in her life—of sex. When he made love to her—if that was what it was, if that was how he thought of it—he gave all those feelings room to expand, like those tiny toy sponges packed away in gelatin capsules that, with the application of hot water, released and actualized. This sense of becoming was what she'd been looking for.

His phone on the night stand shattered the peace, vibrating against the wood. "Go away," he told it.

"You can get it."

"I don't want to."

But he rolled over and grabbed the phone. She missed him, the heat and strength, his touch on her hair, his breath on her ear.

"Oh, crap. It's the network." He tapped to answer. "Hello?" His voice shifted, became deeper, more serious. Professional.

She lay back on the pillow, staring at the ceiling.

"Hello, sir." He sat up, tugging the sheet to cover himself.

There was a long silence at Brett's end. She could hear only a flutter of sound coming from the other end of the line. He listened, his posture rigid. She began to feel afraid. The longer he was silent, the more afraid she felt.

"I know," he said finally. "And I don't want to make any excuses for it. I know we talked about how important a dignified image was, and I know this is the last thing the network wanted to see from me. I'm very sorry. Nothing like this will ever happen again."

More silence. He didn't turn to look at her, didn't signal her, didn't seem to remember she was there. Probably he wished she weren't there. Brett had always compartmentalized the pieces of his life—the professional from the personal, the romantic from the rest—possibly that was why he could never include a woman in anything that mattered to him.

He must be talking to his new boss. Most likely the network had seen the brouhaha about Celine and was not pleased. She couldn't really blame them. No matter what role Brett had played in his own fate, no matter how much he was responsible for the situation he'd gotten himself into, it would be terrible for him to lose his job over it. There was enough collateral damage already.

Brett spoke again, that low, steady voice, the same one he'd used on camera, the one that let New Yorkers know all was well, even if the Burmese python population in Florida was out of control. "I've taken care of it. When I come back to New York, I'm going to be with one woman exclusively. Serious, long-term, someone who people can get used to seeing me with."

I've taken care of it.

Her feet and hands got cold.

Surely he didn't mean that the way it sounded.

Right?

He didn't mean he'd taken up with her on purpose as damage control.

Right?

But she could hear her heart beating in her ears, feel it pounding at her throat and wrists, a trapped thing in her chest. *What if he did?* Because—how convenient that would be for him. How convenient *she* was for him. The perfect solution. As soon as things had gone south with Celine, he must have known the network would hear about it. And he had seen her as an opportunity and pounced.

And she—

Well, she'd be an easy mark, primed as she'd been— *for years*—to fall for him.

She took a deep breath. No. She didn't want to believe it. No one was that shallow or that opportunistic.

He couldn't have said all those things and not meant them. *I never want to stop. I'm not ready to give you up yet.*

She'd felt such a surge of warmth, such a swell of love for him. Such an overwhelming wave of hope.

Except—a moment flashed in her head, in the cab, when he'd had all the right words for Celine. That was him—she'd said it herself—the man with the golden tongue. And those words? She'd said this herself, too— those words didn't have to mean anything bigger than the moment.

Her mind was dark, swirling with panic.

He couldn't have done what he did and not meant it.

Like a last stab at faith.

But he'd done it hundreds if not thousands of other times, exactly this way and for exactly this long, and *not meant it.*

If there was a man who could say it and not mean it, it was Brett Jordan.

She made herself get out of the bed and put on her clothes, as he finished up the call. She didn't hear what he said, the words lost in the grim clench of her fear. She pulled on her panties and her pants, her bra and her tank top. She twisted up her hair and tied it in a knot.

She had her hand on the doorknob when he set down his phone. "Where are you going?" he asked, and there was something light in his voice. He was happy. Of course he was. He had gotten a stay of execution.

"To pack."

"No. Stay and celebrate! I'm keeping my job, at least for now."

"Glad to have been of some use to you." The words felt like ice chips on her tongue.

He narrowed his eyes at her. "Lise. What's going on?"

She had to get away from him and away from herself. She had to give herself some room to think, to push back the heavy panic and make some sense of things. She slipped out the door, trying to push it shut behind her. He blocked it with his body, though, so she left it and fled down the hall.

He must have stopped only long enough to pull on shorts, because a moment later he dashed after her.

She pounded the elevator button with her thumb. *Down, down, down. Get me out of here.* Her thoughts had slowed and become elemental.

He stopped behind her. "C'mon, Lise. Tell me what's going on?"

She took a deep breath. "Nothing. I'm—" *I'm freaking out. I'm being crazy.* You *make me crazy.*

"Whatever you think you heard me say on the phone—"

"You said you'd taken care of it. You said—" She was breathing hard. This is what she'd always been afraid of. This. This exactly. That one day her resolve would slip, and she would let him in. Then she would become a notch on his bedpost, and she would grasp and cling and flail but not be able to hold on to him.

She was just like the others. No better. No different. And Brett would always be Brett.

"You said, 'I've taken care of it.' Like I was something on a checklist."

The words, spoken out loud, sounded so lunatic that she wanted to take them back. Shovel them into her mouth and clamp down.

He wasn't looking at her like he thought she was crazy. He was looking at her with her own panic echoed in his eyes. "No. It's not like that. You know it's not."

"I *don't* know. I don't. That's the thing. That's the point."

"Lise, I swear, I didn't mean it like that."

She wanted to believe him. She *should* believe him.

She gave up on the elevator and strode for the stairs.

He caught up with her again, grabbed her arm. Twisted her around, hard. It hurt her shoulder, and she cried out.

"I'm sorry!" His eyes flashed surprise and alarm.

Laughter floated up to them, then footfalls, and they both froze. A couple came into view, their heads inclined toward each other, sharing low, intimate words. She flinched from it. The laughter and the conversation stopped when the couple spotted her and Brett, and she knew the space between them was charged with misery.

The couple moved past them silently.

We've infected them, she thought.

"It's not like that." He reached for her once more, his grip still too hard on her arms. "My wanting to be with you in New York has *nothing* to do with my job. *Nothing.*"

She'd hurt him, maybe made him angry. She could see it in the dark flash of his eyes and the set of his jaw.

"You have to believe that." He shook her a little for emphasis. "Please, come on. Do you think I could fake that? What we just did? Put on an act like that, just to convince you to play my serious girlfriend? Is that how little you think of me? Jesus!"

He let her go, and she took a step back.

"Maybe I don't have much relationship stamina," he said. "Maybe I'm not obvious boyfriend material. But I've never lied to a woman about how I felt, or what I wanted from her."

He turned away from her, and she saw that the cords in his neck stood out, that his hands were fisted. She heard his breath now, coming hard, the same way it did when they made love.

Her own breath sped up in response, and she hated herself for that. She was weak and needy. When she got out of here, she would find a way to get rid of that need, to totally erase it from who she was.

He tried to take her hand. She yanked it away.

"Lise." His face softened.

"I was always in love with you." After all these years, it was a great relief to say it, but at the same time, it made her terribly sad. Because it was too little, too late. "I fell in love with you the first night I met you. Before. Forever ago. In college. When we played Scrabble."

He was surprised. Of course he was. She had been a genius at hiding her feelings. She had buried them so deep that most of the time she had not known how she felt.

"All those years, I was waiting. I waited until it wore a rut in my brain. But I was okay with that. That wasn't the worst part. The worst part was—"

It was the look on his face now that she hated. Sympathy. Bordering on pity. But she couldn't stop. She'd never said this part out loud, not even to herself. "When it finally happened. And I let myself think— and then—"

He opened his mouth, and she could tell he was going to apologize again, so she cut him off. "Stop. I know you're sorry. But you're sorry for all the wrong things. You're sorry you went out with Julie. But what about the fact that after we kissed that night, you acted like it never happened? How do you think that made me feel?"

"I—"

"That kiss—"

But she couldn't say it. Even now, two years later, despite everything that had passed between them, that kiss was something sacred to her. Something he'd given her and then taken away. She'd had him, and he'd snatched himself away, and she could not forgive him or forget the pain or convince herself that it would not happen again.

She turned away, not wanting him to see the tears welling. For a moment, she hovered. It would be so easy to take what he offered, to hang on for as long as she could. But her panic during that phone call, her misery now and her edge-of-reasonable behavior, had told her that she couldn't. For her, there was no "then" and "now." There was only the way she'd always felt. And she couldn't do this again. Not the waiting, not the daring to hope, and not the part that came after. The moment when she realized that, for him, nothing had happened. Nothing would.

"It's not you," she said quietly. "It's me. I can't. I can't do it."

"Could you just try? One more time?" She almost couldn't hear him.

"I did try, but you see how it is. I'm a mess. I'm not usually like this, but you make me like this. *I* make me like this, around you."

He cupped his open hand around a clenched fist. His knuckles were white, the muscles in his arms ropy and tense. She wouldn't let herself look at him, not at the planes of his stomach and chest, and not at what she knew had to be the pleading in his eyes. "I don't know what to say." His voice was low, rough, and so different from the tone he'd used on the phone. All of his certainty had been washed away in the flood of her emotions. "I've told you how I feel about you. I'm… This is big for me. I don't say those things to anyone. And I've sworn I'll never hurt you again. I feel like I'm offering you everything I have to offer. I don't know what else to say."

She didn't speak, but she let herself look at him, at his beautiful green eyes, the crease between his brows, the slight downturn of his mouth, which even now, she wanted to lean close and taste.

"That's the problem, right?" he said. "It's not enough. I'm not enough."

She wanted to say, again, "It's not you," but the thing was, the truth was, he was exactly right. What he could offer was not enough to silence her fears.

He waited, his eyes searching her face.

She shook her head. "I couldn't ever trust you."

The words echoed in the stairwell.

He turned away first.

She watched him for a moment, taking in the long, strong line of his neck; the muscles in his back that bunched, even when he was relatively still, with tension. Even now she wanted to ease her fingers into his soft hair. How easy it would be to take a step toward him, weave her fingers through his hair, rest her face against the broad, hard surface of his back. And he'd turn in her arms—she knew he would.

She fled down the stairs.

18

By the time Elisa had been back in New York for a week, the scandal had run its course—a few splashes of excitement on the internet, some blathering on the nightly entertainment shows, one photographic spread in a glossy weekly. Elisa had fielded many phone calls, even a few invitations to appear on TV, but at Haven's request, she'd declined any comment or appearance. Any attempt to explain what happened that weekend would sound like blame-dodging, and that—even more than a botched boot camp weekend—would sully her business.

There were no pictures of her and Brett in the spreads or on the shows, as if they hadn't been there at all. Sometimes when she opened a magazine and found not a single picture of her and Brett standing inappropriately close, she was disappointed.

Rendezvous was—well, it just was. Despite her own sense of failure, nothing dramatic *happened*. No one called her to tell her they were taking their business elsewhere. She actually got a few calls and emails from potential new clients who said they'd heard about her through the entertainment weeklies. Apparently they'd been more intrigued by the concept of a dating coach than disturbed by Elisa's failure to reform the unreformable. She supposed it was further proof that there was no such thing as bad publicity.

She welcomed the new clients, met with them, did their intake interviews. But the truth was, she didn't have the stomach for it. She was weepy and exhausted. She'd made her big bid for fame, and it had fallen flat. The situation might have been easier to handle if it had gone up in flames. Instead, she was left with her life, exactly as it had been before she'd flown to the Caribbean.

Well, not exactly as it had been. There was an absence that hadn't been there before. Forcing herself not to think about Brett and the dozen small ways he'd rescued her, the tenderness with which he'd said her name and touched her hair, or how she'd felt as he'd moved inside her, was a full-time, all-out, whole-body effort. She had to be constantly vigilant, or the scent of early flowers as she passed a brownstone garden would knock her backward and leave her stunned.

It was her life, as it had been, only now it was loaded with minefields, and she tiptoed carefully around herself, stiff and awkward.

She had one more loose end to tie up from the weekend. She picked up the phone and called Morrow. They exchanged pleasantries and agreed on a kill fee for the videos, and then she said, "I can put your check in the mail, but I know you're not far from here, and if you want to come pick it up, that's fine, too. I'm sorry it's taken me so long. I've been—busy."

"Could use the walk. You be there another hour?"

She would, she told him, and they hung up.

She sat at her desk, but instead of focusing on the new workshop she was supposed to lead next weekend, she checked Twitter. Although she found the social media platform overwhelming, she'd begun tweeting here and there, tips and suggestions, mainly. Meanwhile, she'd been avoiding Facebook like the plague. The other day, as if to add insult to injury, Facebook had suggested again that she might want to be friends with Brett. "No," she'd said aloud. "I don't want to be friends with you. I don't even want to be reminded that you exist."

There was a knock on the outer office door, and she called Morrow in. He stood in front of her desk. "Hey," he grunted.

"Hi there." She took the check from her pocket and handed it to him.

"Thanks."

"You're welcome. It was good working with you. Do you have an email address I can reach you at if I have other work for you?"

"Sure. Tomorrowsvideo at greatmail dot com."

She found a pad and pen and started to write it down. She got as far as the *M* when her hand stalled, and she looked up at him. "Tomorrow's Video, like Tomorrow's News?"

Morrow's facial expression got twitchy.

Her stomach twisted. Upon returning to New York, there hadn't been nasty surprises waiting for her around every corner. Life had been surprisingly, almost stultifyingly, ordinary. But here was the other shoe, ready to drop.

"Morrow, did you send all those tweets about Celine?" She almost didn't want to know. She wasn't sure she had the energy to care.

"Shouldn't have. Panicked."

"What?"

"Thought you'd broken the exclusive. Wanted to get something out there before that other guy did. Sorry. Should've had more faith."

She stared at his pimply, bald head and lime green polo shirt. This—this—vile little man…

"You're Tomorrowsnews."

"To Morrow's News." He said it in a tone that skated disturbingly close to proud.

She'd hired this guy, invited him into her weekend, given him an exclusive, and *this* was how he'd repaid her?

He'd tweeted horrible things about Celine as if he were Steve. He'd tricked them all, even caused Haven to leave her sick mom and fly to St. Barts. Maybe Elisa wouldn't have been able to put the weekend back together, but Morrow's actions had made it 100 percent certain that there had been no chance.

She had to take a deep breath because, if she didn't, she was going to throttle the life out of his fat, pimply throat.

"You are the scum on the bottom of my shoe after a full day of trudging around New York," she said. "Get out of here."

"Please don't tell anyone."

"Out."

"Should give this back." Morrow extended the check. She wouldn't extend her hand to take it. He left it on the desk. Then he put something down on top of it, something small and gray, before slinking away. "Sorry. So sorry."

Poor Steve. She'd been colossally, impossibly, outrageously wrong. She'd falsely accused an innocent man and ruined a relationship. If there had been a Hippocratic oath for dating coaches, she would have broken it.

She picked up the check and the small gray object. A thumb drive. Morrow had written on it in permanent marker, "St. Barts, Celine Carr."

The footage from the weekend. The wreckage of her promo video, of her aspirations.

Of her heart.

She balanced the thumb drive in the palm of her hand.

One broken heart was enough. She still had a chance to redeem herself.

She picked up the phone.

STEVE FLYNN HAD a website, and his website had a phone number, and he answered the phone on the third ring. "Hey."

"I am the last person you want to talk to," Elisa said. Might as well get the prostrating and groveling over with.

"For $500, is that Elisa Henderson at the other end of the line?"

He hadn't hung up. That was good. And shocking. "Yeah, it's me."

"Have you called with a really excellent reason why I should talk to you? Because I am very hard pressed to think of one."

"I—I'm calling to apologize. I know it's too little, too late but—"

"She won't take my calls. She won't communicate with me in any way, shape or form. I can't even convince her publicist to pass her a note."

Elisa wanted to cry, not out of self-pity but for this guy she'd so thoroughly wronged. She and Haven had been his judge, jury and executioner.

"Can you tell me this? Do you think it was me? Do you really think I would do that to her?"

"I—I'm—there's no excuse. I misjudged you, I leaped to conclusions. I'm sorry. I did think it was you."

This was harder than she'd thought. She had to face up to the part of her that had been so willing to believe the worst of him.

"Why?"

Because she'd watched, powerless, as her teenaged sister's boyfriends had made Julie cry, month after month, year after year. Because Brett had strung women together like beads on a cheap necklace. And yet, not because of either of those things.

She'd been willing to think the worst of Steve because at some point she'd chosen to believe that men were jerks until proven otherwise.

"I screwed up," she said.

He made a sound at the other end of the phone. It might have been exasperation, because she wasn't answering the question he was asking. He wanted to know about the chain of events that had led her and Haven to indict him.

"Look, it's not an excuse," she said. "I'm not defending my leap to judgment at all. But just so you know what's out there—Haven told me you posted stuff to Razzle all the time. That a celebrity you'd posted had gotten sexually assaulted, and that you were—not sorry."

"Christ," he said. "Wow. Okay, so, yeah, it's true that I posted a couple of photos, when I first started taking pictures. Just a couple. And a woman did claim that she'd been assaulted because of me. But it wasn't true. It turned out she'd made up the story to get attention. You can look it up. There was a whole piece about it in one of the entertainment weeklies." She heard him draw a deep breath. "It is really a total jungle out there. Once you're on the web, nothing ever goes away, not even the versions that aren't true. And by the way? I never post to those sites these days. I mean, I can totally see that it's an awful idea to give away celebrity locations. I just try to get good photos."

She was rapidly searching via the Google site as he spoke, and there it was, the whole story, complete with the fact that Steve had been cleared of all wrongdoing. Her chest tightened for him, for all the anger he must have faced down, and the times he'd lost his temper in the wake of it. She wouldn't have done any better. None of them would have.

"I'm sorry you went through that," she said, "and I'm really, really sorry I rushed to judgment about you."

There was a long silence at the other end of the phone. He wasn't quite ready to forgive her, and she understood that.

He sighed. "But there's more, right? I mean, it wasn't just that you'd heard that story from Haven. There was something specific that made you think I was doing wrong by Celine. What happened?"

She told him, about the email and all the tweets from @Tomorrowsnews, although she didn't identify Morrow by name. She hated the videographer's guts, but she didn't want Steve to go to jail for his murder.

She told him about that one terribly intimate, incriminating tweet.

"It's true," he said thoughtfully. "The whimpering is the sexiest thing."

"It's probably true of a lot of women. It was a lucky guess. And if he was wrong, only a few people would know, right?" It had been clever, the work of a guy who probably wrote fiction in his spare time and knew the power of a telling detail.

"I need to talk to her. Can you help me?"

She took a deep breath. "I do have this one idea."

"I thought you might. Does it require me to forgive you? Because I'm still pissed."

"No," she said. "Stay pissed. As long as you need to. But it does require a little public humiliation. How are you with that?"

"Totally fine. Especially if it involves public humiliation for you, too."

"Definitely."

"Tell me what I need to do."

19

NEW YORK HAD changed while Brett was away in the Caribbean. It was darker and colder, louder and smellier. The buildings blocked out the sky in a way he hadn't noticed in a long time. He'd left the relative warmth of the subway, and an icy breeze knifed up the narrow street and penetrated his thin quilted jacket. Ten days ago he'd been in paradise, but now he was cast out. To make things worse, he'd been summoned to account for himself and meet with his new boss at the network.

That didn't bode well, but he couldn't care in the way he thought he should. He could think about only the steady beat of absence in his head and his heart. *Elisa.*

So much had gone wrong, and it was a deep, fixed misery. He wanted her not just in his frustrated, aching cock but in his gut, his chest, his *fingertips* for God's sake. There were more hollow empty spaces in his body than he'd known existed. He kept seeing her face when she'd said, "I couldn't ever trust you."

What could you say to that?

The building where the network's offices were housed stuck into the gray sky like a clean glass spike. He loved the way a building like that in New York could exist right across the street from arches and gargoyles and old stone, the two of them challenging each other over the hurrying pedestrians.

He slipped through the spike's revolving doors, ran the gauntlet of lobby security, then took a high-speed elevator to the twenty-ninth floor. Brett's new boss, Hank Ormond, met him just inside the network's bulletproof glass doors, offering him a cup of coffee and shaking his hand. Ormond was an ex-football player, square edged and chiseled, like a dark-haired Howie Long. Brett had done a lot of research on Ormond before taking the job. Everyone liked him, and he was known for being tough but fair.

Ormond gestured to a chair at the enormous, glossy-topped conference table and took a seat beside Brett. Ormond's big frame made his chair look spindly and inadequate. Brett felt spindly and inadequate, too.

"I'm not going to sugarcoat this. The guys upstairs are *not* happy. You're not even on the air yet, and you're a distraction. They were afraid of this from the beginning, and I talked them into taking a chance on you. They wanted the older guy, the established guy, the family guy. I said, no, you could handle this."

"I can handle this."

"A news anchor's biggest job is to be trustworthy. Dependable. You have to avoid not only outright scandal but even the scent of scandal. This job is 99 percent image. We talked about that in the interview. You said—I quote—'Happy to be a pretty face.'"

He'd meant it, too.

In St. Barts, on the balcony, he'd told Elisa the same thing. *I'm more the glitz guy.*

And she'd said, *You put yourself down a lot, you know that?... What's that about?*

What *was* that about?

He wasn't that guy. He brimmed self-confidence. Oozed it. Always had. He knew he was good-looking. He knew women loved him. He knew he was the best guy for this anchor job. Ormond had seen it, too. Authoritative, easy on the eyes…

But not just that.

Right?

Not just a pretty face.

Elisa thought he was more. And she wanted him to believe it, too.

Ormond was watching him, waiting.

"I have a question for you. About the reporting."

"What reporting?"

"How much I'll be doing."

"You know we have a team for that. You need to focus on how you come across. That's your job."

"It's nonnegotiable? If I work here, I won't be shaping coverage?"

"We've got a great reporting staff. Some networks want more investigative work from their anchors. That's not our model. We could throw you a bone every now and again…"

Like a dog, he thought. Like a *show* dog.

Glitz. Substance.

If you were my client—

He had not let Elisa finish that sentence because he didn't want to be psychoanalyzed. He hadn't wanted to hear her talk about self-esteem or tell him that the reason he dated women like it was going out of style was that he didn't think highly enough of himself.

But it was true, wasn't it? That, in the end, he hadn't gone after the NPR and the *New York Times* jobs.

"Jordan?" Ormond's face was creased with concern.

"I'm trying to be as straight with you here as I can. I'm telling you exactly what we want from you. We need a pretty face, and we need you squeaky clean behind the ears. Can you do that? Because we need to know right now. This is officially a zero-tolerance situation. One wrong move and you're out."

Being a pretty face no longer seemed enough, and it was because of Elisa's faith in him; her persistent, relentless need to push him to live up to standards he hadn't dared to hold himself to.

If you were my client—

He didn't want to be her client. But he no longer hated the way she made him doubt. Far from it. He loved that about her, that she wouldn't let him settle.

And not just that. He loved everything about her, her auburn hair and light brown eyes, wide mouth, luminous skin, life-changing smile. Her rolling on the floor with laughter over something he'd said during a Scrabble game. Her quick sense of humor, her mile-deep stubborn streak. She was such a hard-ass. God, he loved that about her, the way she'd light into him and keep him honest.

He loved her.

Maybe he'd never convince her of that, but he would die trying. And in the meantime he was going to show her that he knew his own worth, because that was the best way to prove he knew hers.

He took a deep breath. "I can't do it, Ormond. It's not me."

Ormond scowled. "How hard is it, Jordan? Keep it in your pants."

"No, not that part. The pretty face. I don't want to be that guy. I want a job that uses my reporting chops. Something with some investigative teeth."

Ormond's face darkened. "That's not how we do it around here," he said.

"That's not how you've done it in the past. I respect that. But I'd like you to give this way a chance."

"You're not in a position to bargain with us right now. Given we had some doubts to begin with. Given that you've already managed to get the network bad publicity."

"No," Brett agreed. "I'm not in a position to bargain."

He kept all hint of threat out of his voice. This wasn't meant to be an ultimatum, even though he knew in his heart that he would walk away. Not from their low expectations of him but from his own. He could do better, and he owed it to Elisa—

No, he owed it to himself.

"If you can't give me serious reporting time, I won't work here."

Ormond regarded him levelly. "Jordan, I'm telling you I can't. And you're telling me that means you're out? No contract, no network anchor job."

Brett nodded.

"That's your final answer?"

Elisa had sometimes said that to him when they were playing Scrabble, because he liked to keep his fingers on the tiles for a minute after he played them, to see if he could spot something better. She used to say it just like a game show host, all drama. Leaning in, narrowing her eyes.

The memory made him smile, and Ormond looked at him like he was stark raving mad.

"Yes," he said. "That's my final answer."

ELISA AND STEVE sat side by side on her couch, his laptop resting on the coffee table in front of them, watching

Morrow's footage. Elisa was surprised by how much there was. Morrow had been everywhere, a stealthy, constant presence. In the airport. In the resort lobby. At the pool, the camera steady on Elisa's and Brett's serious faces as they conversed over Celine's sleeping form. In the bar, Morrow had captured every last nuance of Brett's drinks with Celine and all the unsubtle sexual chemistry of Celine and Steve's performance. Morrow had continued to roll the camera long after Celine's fall, capturing the moment when Brett had shoved Steve, the fury on Brett's face, and the matching shock on Steve's and Elisa's. The camera had followed them out of the bar, the footage snapping to blue when they were no longer visible.

And most shockingly, Morrow had stayed on the beach after their conversation, because he'd captured every interaction that she and Brett had had from that point on, almost until they closed the door of Brett's room to make love. There was very little audio, at least very little that would be usable, but Elisa was a matchmaker, and she could read everything in body language, including Steve and Celine's genuine affection for each other and Celine's own single-mindedness. Only Brett was a mystery to Elisa, his expression often bland as he watched events unfold.

Steve clicked again on the frame where he sat on the beach with his arm wrapped around Celine, holding her close. He leaned forward, staring at the screen.

"You okay?" Elisa asked.

"I'm in love with her."

She smiled at him. He had a crooked smile, brilliantly white teeth, dark skin and long, thin eyebrows that kept his face from being movie-star handsome. From a physical perspective, he and Celine were the perfect opposites-attract couple. They would have made a beautiful marketing photo for Rendezvous, angel light and devil dark. The thought hardly stung.

"I was in love with her almost from the very beginning." Steve said it so quietly and simply that it hurt to hear it.

He touched the spot on the screen where Celine's hair was frozen as it blew in the wind. "It's hard to exactly explain what it is about her. She's got this—this *glow,* like she's lit from within. I can't take my eyes off her." He said it almost apologetically. "And I had fun with her. The karaoke, the beach, paddleboarding, the sex, everything. It's been a tough couple of years for me. I think I'd gotten kind of bitter, and she snapped me out of it. I felt—purified. Is that crazy? Totally peaceful and clean. Makes no sense. I know."

Elisa's eyes prickled. There was an odd, sweet buoyancy in her chest, the feeling she got when she heard about someone falling head over heels or meeting a long-lost loved one. The feeling brought with it the threat of a certain kind of tears, the kind that went with being human and getting a chance to witness unadulterated happiness.

Steve had also showed Elisa prints of his still photos, and they were spread out on the glass-topped table, shot after shot of Celine, laughing, frowning, pouting, framed by the ocean, the beautiful St. Barts's flowers, the white-and-red buildings, the blue sky. Steve and Celine were a love story, and she'd been too busy with her own woes to revel in it. Some matchmaker she was.

"I don't know if she feels the same way," he admitted. "I know I'm not the only guy who wants to date her. I should probably just get in line." He shoved his fingers through his hair, raking it off his forehead.

"No. You shouldn't." Elisa clicked on a single frame, right out of the middle of Steve and Celine's performance. "Look at her."

There it was, on Celine's face, that same brief glimpse of perfect happiness. She did look like she'd been lit from within, and it wasn't a look Elisa had seen Celine wear very many times. Her joy was because of Steve. How funny that was, that the thing that attracted him to her was the intensity with which she was attracted to him. Elisa had felt it, too, with Brett—

She wasn't going to think about that.

"She *is* an actress," he pointed out.

"She wasn't acting."

"How do you know?"

She pressed her palm into her denim-clad thigh, biting her bottom lip. "Because I saw her face when she thought you'd written those tweets."

"She was really upset?"

"She was devastated."

He looked back at the frame on the screen, and she watched his smile creep back, lighting him up. "I want her to look at me like that again. Preferably at least once a day—for the foreseeable future." He sighed. "Possibly for the rest of my life."

She must have signaled her doubt somehow, because he said quickly, "I know you can't promise me that. That part's my job. But I'm game to give this a shot."

She smiled at him and patted his arm. "I'm glad to hear it."

"What about you and Brett?"

Startled, she met his probing gaze, then had to look away. "What about us?"

"You guys are together, right?"

God, the last thing she wanted to do right now was

talk about her and Brett. "There wasn't ever anything between us. Not really."

"Seriously?" Steve stared at her for a moment. And then he leaned forward and began clicking through video frames. "Tell me you don't see it."

She looked, unwillingly. He'd stopped on a frame in which she and Brett were ascending the stairs from the beach. Where the hell had Morrow stood to capture that footage? He was a better stealth videographer than she had guessed. Creep.

In this particular frame, she and Brett held hands, and she gazed ahead up the stairs, more or less toward the camera. But Brett wasn't looking at the camera. Brett was staring at her. She had seen him eye her many times that weekend with a dark, covetous look that had set her hair on fire. This was different. This—

"You see?" Steve demanded.

There it was, that reaction she couldn't hide. The thrill of knowing, of seeing, that people could feel that way about each other, that amid everything bad that went on in the world, there was this kind of transcendence. She could deny herself, and she could lie to herself, but in her matchmaker's heart, she knew the look in Brett's eyes when she saw it.

"You see?"

She couldn't take her eyes off the still. He was looking at her like she was important, like she was necessary, like she was everything.

Beside her, Steve cleared his throat, and she turned.

"I don't know what happened between you guys, but I think you need to wake up to the fact that he's crazy about you."

For a moment she could only focus on the expanding joy in her chest. Then she remembered and shook her head, and the joy shrank down to a single point of permanent, sharp disappointment. This was Brett they were talking about. Whatever it was that she'd seen in Brett's face didn't matter. "Even if it were true, and I don't necessarily think it is, that guy doesn't know how to commit. I've known him for years, and there isn't a monogamous bone in his body."

"People change."

The echo of Brett's words startled her.

"I should know. I used to be an asshole. I would have done anything to succeed at one point, and then—" He turned away. "I did things I wasn't proud of. You know what they were, which is why you leaped to the conclusions you did."

People change.

Brett had been talking about Steve when he'd said that. And he'd been right that Steve's motives were pure. He'd been right that a person who did something less than admirable was not doomed to repeat the mistake.

Steve was still talking. "I probably would have drawn the same conclusions you did. At least back then, I know I would have. I was totally incapable of believing that people were anything other than the sum of their greedy impulses."

"Do you think that's who I am? Do you think I'm like that?"

He made an incredulous face. "Why are you asking me?"

People change.

Brett could change. But more to the point, *she* could change. All those years ago, when she had not been able to make the leap beyond friendship with him, had that been about him or about her? Had she ever really given him a chance? That night after they'd been to Aquarium, when possibility had slipped into reality, had she fought for what she wanted? Or had she turned away, already having decided that it could never work?

She no longer knew for sure. But she did know that long before that moment, she had failed to trust him or to risk herself. From the moment she'd met him, she'd let her fear that he'd break her be stronger than her faith in him as a friend. She'd held herself so far away that he could never hurt her.

She, not he, had made sure that nothing real could ever happen between them.

Even if she'd gone after him, and he'd rejected her, *that* at least would have been real and honest. If she'd called him on how much his sleeping with Julie had hurt her or told him why, their friendship might very well have continued. Instead, she had walked away without ever risking herself. She had guaranteed that nothing, not even the scraps of their friendship, could survive.

What the hell had happened to her? To the girl who'd told Brett "I can't wait to see what happens next?" When had she become such a coward?

She'd accused him of not thinking highly enough of himself, but it had been her job as his friend to see beyond his games and self-protecting shell, and she hadn't had the courage to do it.

Are you with me? Because if you're not with me, you're against me.

Now she saw. From the very beginning, she'd been against him. She'd been against *them*.

It hurt her heart to think of the wasted time and possibility. The words that had not even made it into her tight throat but had died in the back of her mind. The kiss she'd conspired to pretend into nonexistence. And now he was out there somewhere believing that he was not worth her trust, when that was the opposite of the truth. She didn't deserve the second chance he'd given her.

But maybe she could. Maybe she could still redeem herself.

People change.

She took a deep breath.

Steve was setting aside clips in the workspace. She touched his arm. "Show me that bit again."

He glanced over. "Which bit?"

"The one where Brett looks at me like he wants to eat me up."

Steve laughed. "Attagirl."

As he pulled up the clip in question, she tried to corral the words hovering in her head. She said them out loud.

"The one where he looks at me like he's in love with me."

20

SHE GOT BRETT'S address from a mutual college friend. He lived on the Upper West Side near the park, and she climbed the front stairs to his apartment building with her heart pounding. She didn't really believe he would turn her away, but she didn't know for sure. Trusting him to love her didn't mean she thought he was sitting alone in his apartment pining for her. He could be entertaining another woman. Or out, drowning his sorrows, assuming he had sorrows on the same scale she did.

She had to do this. That was what it meant to have faith in this. Faith in him. She had to shut out doubts and throw herself headlong into their relationship. What had he said to her on the beach? *Love isn't safe. It's a disaster. It's a tightrope walk without a net. You think you can be the net, but what you're doing is taking all the thrill out of the walk.*

Well, here was the rope, the thrill and the long plunge if she was wrong.

She'd been standing with her finger poised above the buzzer for a long time, maybe a whole minute.

"I can't wait to see what happens next," said a wry voice behind her.

She spun. He'd quietly opened the entrance door to the building and was leaning against the wall. He was wearing an olive-green sweater and well-worn jeans, and she wanted to throw herself at him and breathe him in.

"What are you doing here?" she demanded instead.

"I live here."

"Right." She closed her eyes. "I mean. I don't what know what I mean."

"I think you stole my line. What are *you* doing here?" He adjusted a messenger bag slung across his chest. No one should look as good as he did right now. She had segued almost instantly from fight-or-flight to flat-on-her-back mode. He had always had that effect on her. Always would.

"I came to see you."

"That's pretty funny, because I just came from your apartment, where you weren't, because you were here. Isn't there a scene in *Winnie the Pooh* just like this?"

She nodded. Her heart was beating so hard it hurt her chest. All the words she'd planned and rehearsed had gone right out of her head.

"I brought Scrabble." He withdrew his travel board from his messenger bag. It was the same ratty old plastic board they'd played on years ago. She took it, and relief and excitement scrambled free inside her. "I thought I might be able to convince you to play. And then I thought I might be able to convince you to let me stay. And then I thought I might be able to convince you that I'm serious about becoming a better man. I quit my job."

"What?"

"My glitzy job. You were right. I don't think very highly of myself. I don't actually trust myself to be good at much besides being eye candy."

"You're very good at being eye candy, though," she murmured, because she had to do something to distract herself from the sensations inside her, a joy so sweet it hurt. He was doing it. Leaping hurdles and saying screw the consequences. *Because of her.*

"Don't—you'll get me off topic, and I'll never get to say what I need to say to you. The point is, you make me want to deserve you."

"Don't be ridiculous," she said testily. "Of course you deserve me. If anything, it's the other way around. I don't deserve you. I had so little faith in you, I wouldn't even give you a chance. I might have a little problem with seeing the best in human nature."

"Which is really a terrible trait in a dating coach."

"It is," she agreed. "Completely awful. So I'm officially renouncing it and becoming a hopeless romantic instead."

"Don't do that." He brushed his thumb over her cheek. "I like you cynical and pissy. And it'll help you differentiate yourself in the market. 'Most dating coaches see the best in people—I'll totally hold all your flaws against you and convince the best matches not to have anything to do with you because you're a jerk.'"

"I wasn't *that* bad."

Now his fingers were moving through her hair, making her shiver. "Just that weekend. I think I brought it out in you. But I want to bring out the best in you, like you do in me. You make me want to be the best man I can be, and no one has ever done that before. I can't give it up. I'll never give it up."

She was going to cry, and she hadn't even gotten to the important part. "I'm not doing a good job saying what I came to say."

"I think you're doing an excellent job."

"I was supposed to say, 'I figured out that you're

right. People can change. I'm so sorry I didn't see it sooner, but I believe you can change. That you *have* changed.'"

She had to stop, because the open, *wrecked* look on his face made her tears come, fast and free.

"Stop. You're going to make me cry, too, and you know my masculinity can't handle that. Come here." He held out his arms to her, and she walked into them. Then she couldn't keep crying because it felt too good, and she was very busy trying to collect all her thoughts, and then she wasn't doing that either because he was kissing her. Hard. His mouth was warm and soft, and his hands moved as though he were doing an inventory, making sure she was still all there.

He scooped her in his arms and carried her up two flights of stairs, the Scrabble board clutched in one hand.

"I'm too big for this," she protested, but she didn't want to struggle and throw him off balance.

"You're not. You're light as a feather. Do you know one of the things I love about your body? This is thing one of about ten thousand. I love that you are skinny and soft at the same time."

"Skinny is not a good word," she said.

"No, it's a really good word. You have the most beautiful cheekbones and collarbones and finger bones—"

"Finger bones are also not good words."

"Whatever. And I love that I can see the way you are made, because it is an architectural marvel. But then you are still so soft, I can bury myself in you."

That sent a surge of heat through her, and she turned her face and pressed it against his chest, wanting to bite.

He set her down, fumbled for his key and unlocked the door. "Come sit," he said.

The apartment was small but lovely, with high ceilings and a brick wall with a fireplace and a new kitchen with a granite island and a Viking stove. He gestured to a brown sofa in front of the fireplace, and she sat and put Scrabble on the coffee table. She tucked herself up at one end of the sofa, the way she always had.

He set down the messenger bag but stayed upright. "I still haven't said what I came to say, either. I mean, what I went to your apartment to say. Your friend Sandy messaged me the address on Facebook. It was quite the battle. I had to explain a lot of what had happened in the meantime, and even then she was threatening me with bodily harm if I hurt you again."

She laughed. "Your friend Carl emailed me yours. He also wasn't too eager. I didn't tell him the story, but I did say that things had changed rather radically between us, and there was some unfinished business."

"Good to know our privacy is well protected by our friends. Listen, as much as I know you don't want to hear it, I have something to say to you about Julie."

All the levity had gone out of his voice. He turned half away from her and spoke to the kitchen.

"I went after her because I was scared. I wanted you so much, and that night—oh, my God, Elisa, that night when we kissed? It was the most I'd ever wanted anyone. And not just sex. All that night, all that weird blue light, and I had this crazy sense of possibility that you'd see beyond who I'd been up to that point—"

Her eyes filled with tears again.

"That you'd see only who I was when I was with you." He paced as he spoke and up to that moment he hadn't been looking at her, but when he said that, he looked right at her. And held her gaze. His eyes were so full of warmth and love that she couldn't look away.

"I was buoyant. It was like floating. But then I freaked out. I knew I had nothing to give you except disappointment. But instead of telling you that and begging you to help me be a better man, I did something stupid. I was scared and doing that stupid thing kept you at a distance. That's why I went after Julie. So I wouldn't sleep with you. Only—in the end, she wasn't you. Only the palest imitation. I couldn't do it. I know you were mad about it, no matter what you say now." He sat down on the opposite end of the sofa.

"Hell, yes, I was mad," she said. "I was—"

"You don't have to say it. I broke your heart. I broke mine, too. I convinced myself that I was exactly that guy I thought I was. And then I proceeded to be him. Until the weekend in St. Barts, and you, and—so I get it, Lise. I get why trusting me doesn't seem like a good bet."

"Brett—"

"You don't have to trust me all at once. Just a little bit at a time. Start with moving a few feet closer on the sofa."

She flung herself across the couch and into his arms. "But I do," she said. "That's what I was going to say earlier before you looked at me like that and made me cry. I trust you've changed. I trust *you*. Not a sofa's worth. Completely."

His arms tightened around her. She put her face against the soft wool of his sweater and felt her tension ease. Like he was drawing it out of her.

"I love you." He said it into her hair, but clearly. No reservation, no holding back in his voice.

"I love you, too."

He leaned down and kissed her cheek. Her nose. Her upper lip. Her lower lip.

She moaned.

"Oh, God, don't *do* that," he said. "I go from reasonably comfortable to having all the blood from my entire body in my cock in like three seconds."

She confirmed this diagnosis. It did feel like it.

"So, Elisa?"

"Yeah?"

"Are you with me? Because, you know, if you're not with me—"

She slipped off the couch and settled her own knees between his. "I don't see why it has to be an either/or thing. I'm against you right now—" she gave an emphatic wiggle "—and I don't hear you complaining I'm not with you."

He kissed her, and they didn't get around to pulling out the Scrabble board for almost an hour.

MUCH LATER, HE SAID, "I saw you and Celine and Steve on TV. How did you pull that off? How did you convince Celine to show up without telling her what was going on?"

The couch was narrow, and if he hadn't had one arm firmly around her, she'd be in danger of slipping off, but neither of them had had the wherewithal to make it to the bedroom. She was okay with that. She was okay with everything.

"I had Haven tell her they were making an appearance for *Broken*."

"The look on her face. For a second I thought she was going to turn and run. And Steve's speech was amazing. Did you tell him to say all that stuff?"

Just tell her exactly what you told me, she'd said to him. *Just tell her how she made you feel.*

And he had, and right there on national television, Celine Carr's eyes had filled with tears. So had Elisa's, but no one had been looking at her. They'd been watching as Steve kissed their golden child and the two of them beamed into each other's faces.

"No," she said. "It was just what he wanted to say to her."

"The footage looked great, too." He stroked her hair back from her face and touched her cheek with one finger, the simple gesture of affection sending a tingle through her whole body.

"Morrow did a good job."

"It was nice of you not to attach his name to the host's description of him as 'the cretinous videographer who almost ruined everything.'"

"I couldn't bring myself to actually rake him across the coals on national TV. Even if it's possible he deserved it."

"You're a better person than I am."

"Uh-uh-uh. None of that."

He laughed. "Fine. You're a better person than *most*. And a great dating coach. You took an impossible situation and made two matches out of it."

"Three," she said.

"Three?"

"Right after the show aired, Steve texted to say he'd gotten a call from a gallery owner who'd been curious about his fine art photography. She offered him a show."

"Sweet! That's definitely three."

"I don't think I can take credit for any of them, though. I think they happened despite me, not because of me. But the world seems to agree with you. My phone has been ringing off the hook ever since that segment aired. I'm going to have to turn half of them down," she said happily.

"That's great, because I'm going to be useless financially. I'm reporting for Truth101, which is essentially an online newspaper. It sure as hell won't make us rich."

"But you like it?"

"I love it. And I don't think I would have figured out how wrong the anchor job was for me without your help. Thank you for having faith in me."

She nuzzled his cheek. He'd shaved before coming to her, and she indulged herself by nibbling his jawline. "Given how well my business is going, I think you could probably afford to spend the rest of your days as a man of leisure."

He kissed her, lingering, teasing, nipping.

"Mmm. More."

He obliged. When they surfaced, he said, "So what are you going to do, about choosing your clientele?"

"I think I have to specialize. You know, like 'young professionals' or 'mature women.'"

He wrapped his arms tighter around her and kissed her hair. She wiggled against the hard length of him. She could go again. She was totally amenable to that. She could make love to him for another few days before she needed to come up for air. Although a pint of Ben & Jerry's and a game of Scrabble would be nice right about now, too.

"So what are you thinking? About which to choose?"

"I'm thinking 'celebrities.' I'm thinking Rendezvous caters to the celeb set." And then when his expression turned horrified, she said, "Kidding!"

"Phew. Don't do that to me. Although—I guess if it means free trips to the Caribbean with you, I'm in." He drew a line of kisses from her temple to the corner of her mouth, then opened his mouth softly over hers and took her breath away.

It took her a moment to be able to talk again. "Celebrities are clearly not my strong suit. I'm thinking, actually, that I want to go back to the old way. Just making really good matches for ordinary women who want lifelong marriages. It's not glamorous, but it's what I'm good at, and it's what I love. And I have some fun news. Haven hired me to be *her* dating coach."

He squinted at her. "Seriously? Haven needs a dating coach?"

"She says the overlap between the public relations skill set and the finding-a-mate-for-life skill set is approximately zero."

"I can see that." He turned Elisa in his arms so he could plant little kisses all over her face. "I guess if you can find a match for me, you can find one for anyone, huh?"

She tsked at him. "Hey. What did I tell you about that self-bashing?"

"Oops. Slipped. You'll have to keep my mouth occupied 'til I learn." He kissed her long and lingeringly on the mouth, his tongue teasing at the seam of her lips. "Mmm," he said. Then he pulled back. "You know what would be good right now? Fresh baked chocolate chip cookies and a game of Scrabble."

"That does sound good." The Ben & Jerry's fantasy transformed into a scoop of vanilla melting over the top of a warm cookie.

"First things first," he said. "First I make you scream my name. Then I'll order hot cookies and skunk you at Scrabble."

She laughed. "You really have forgotten a lot about our past."

"I always won."

She bit his ear lightly. "You keep on believing that."

He groaned. "Maybe I let you win sometimes."

"Why don't you stick with what you're good at?"

"What's that?"

"Making me scream your name."

"I can do that."

So he did. And then she whupped his ass at Scrabble.

* * * * *

REQUEST YOUR FREE BOOKS!
2 FREE NOVELS PLUS 2 FREE GIFTS!

red-hot reads!

YES! Please send me 2 FREE Harlequin® Blaze™ novels and my 2 FREE gifts (gifts are worth about $10). After receiving them, if I don't wish to receive any more books, I can return the shipping statement marked "cancel." If I don't cancel, I will receive 4 brand-new novels every month and be billed just $4.74 per book in the U.S. or $4.96 per book in Canada. That's a savings of at least 14% off the cover price. It's quite a bargain. Shipping and handling is just 50¢ per book in the U.S. and 75¢ per book in Canada.* I understand that accepting the 2 free books and gifts places me under no obligation to buy anything. I can always return a shipment and cancel at any time. Even if I never buy another book, the two free books and gifts are mine to keep forever.

150/350 HDN F4WC

Name _____ (PLEASE PRINT)

Address _____ Apt. #

City _____ State/Prov. _____ Zip/Postal Code

Signature (if under 18, a parent or guardian must sign)

Mail to the Harlequin® Reader Service:
IN U.S.A.: P.O. Box 1867, Buffalo, NY 14240-1867
IN CANADA: P.O. Box 609, Fort Erie, Ontario L2A 5X3

Want to try two free books from another line?
Call 1-800-873-8635 or visit www.ReaderService.com.

* Terms and prices subject to change without notice. Prices do not include applicable taxes. Sales tax applicable in N.Y. Canadian residents will be charged applicable taxes. Offer not valid in Quebec. This offer is limited to one order per household. Not valid for current subscribers to Harlequin Blaze books. All orders subject to credit approval. Credit or debit balances in a customer's account(s) may be offset by any other outstanding balance owed by or to the customer. Please allow 4 to 6 weeks for delivery. Offer available while quantities last.

Your Privacy—The Harlequin® Reader Service is committed to protecting your privacy. Our Privacy Policy is available online at www.ReaderService.com or upon request from the Harlequin Reader Service.

We make a portion of our mailing list available to reputable third parties that offer products we believe may interest you. If you prefer that we not exchange your name with third parties, or if you wish to clarify or modify your communication preferences, please visit us at www.ReaderService.com/consumerchoice or write to us at Harlequin Reader Service Preference Service, P.O. Box 9062, Buffalo, NY 14269. Include your complete name and address.

HB13R2

A SEAL's Salvation

by Tawny Weber

It all began ten years ago....

"Genna, you're crazy. You don't have to do this."

"Of course I do. You dared me." Genna Reilly gave her best friend a wide-eyed look.

She needed to do this. Now, while anticipation was still zinging through her system, making her feel brave enough to take on the world. Or, in this case, to take down the sexiest bad boy of Bedford, California.

She wanted Brody Lane.

But he had practically made a career of ignoring her existence. Time to end that.

So tonight, thanks to Dina's dare, she was going to do something about it.

"I don't kiss and tell," Genna murmured.

"You mean you don't kiss or do anything else," Dina corrected, rolling her eyes.

"The dare was to kiss Brody Lane," Sylvie pointed out, glancing nervously toward the garage. "Genna's not going in there unless she follows through."

Genna looked toward the garage, the silhouette of a man working on a motorcycle.

"If I'm not back in ten minutes, head home," she instructed, fluffing her hair and hurrying off.

Carefully she peeked around the open doorway.

There he was. Brody Lane, in all his bare-chested glory. Black hair fell across his eyes as he bent over the Harley. She had the perfect view of his sexy denim-clad butt.

Genna fanned herself. Oh, baby, he was so hot.

She took a deep breath, then stepped through the doorway.

And waited.

Nothing.

"Hey, Brody," she called out, her voice shaking slightly. "How're you doing?"

His body went still, his head turned. His eyes, golden-brown like a cat's, narrowed.

Slowly, he straightened away from the bike, the light glinting off that sleek golden skin. Her gaze traveled from the broad stretch of his shoulders down his tapered waist to his jeans, slung low and loose on his hips.

Oh, wow.

"Genna?" He cast a glance behind her, then back with an arched brow. "What the hell do you want?"

**Pick up A SEAL'S SALVATION
by Tawny Weber, available wherever you buy
Harlequin® Blaze® books.**

The stakes are high!

Reformed con artist Maddie Howe must revert to her former ways in order to rescue her brother, even if it means kidnapping the hunky U.S. marshal who is hot on her trail! From the Sierra Nevada foothills to the glittering casinos of Reno, Colton Black will go along as her "hostage" in order to keep her safe, even at the risk of losing his badge—and his heart.

Don't miss

Hard to Hold

by *Karen Foley,*
available this February wherever you buy
Harlequin Blaze books.

HARLEQUIN®
™

Blaze®

Red-Hot Reads
www.Harlequin.com